CRETAN TEAT

Brian Aldiss, OBE, is a fiction and science fiction writer, poet, playwright, critic, memoirist and artist. He was born in Norfolk in 1925. After leaving the army, Aldiss worked as a bookseller, which provided the setting for his first book, *The Brightfount Diaries* (1955). His first published science fiction work was the story 'Criminal Record', which appeared in *Science Fantasy* in 1954. Since then he has written nearly 100 books and over 300 short stories, many of which are being reissued as part of The Brian Aldiss Collection.

Several of Aldiss's books have been adapted for the cinema; his story 'Supertoys Last All Summer Long' was adapted and released as the film *AI* in 2001. Besides his own writing, Brian has edited numerous anthologies of science fiction and fantasy stories, as well as the magazine *SF Horizons*.

Aldiss is a vice-president of the International H. G. Wells Society and in 2000 was given the Damon Knight Memorial Grand Master Award by the Science Fiction Writers of America. Aldiss was awarded the OBE for services to literature in 2005.

T0337277

By the same author from The Friday Project

Life in the West
Forgotten Life
Remembrance Day
Somewhere East of Life

The Brightfount Diaries
Bury my Heart at W. H. Smiths
Dracula Unbound
Frankenstein Unbound
Moreau's Other Island
Finches of Mars
This World and Nearer Ones
The Pale Shadow of Science
The Detached Retina
The Primal Urge
Brothers of the Head
The Zodiacal Planet Galaxy
Enemies of the System
Eighty Minute Hour
Comfort Zone
Songs from the Steppes: The Poems of Makhtumkuli
Interpreter

And available exclusively as ebooks
50 x 50: The Mini-sagas
The Horatio Stubbs Trilogy
The Squire Quartet
The Monster Trilogy

BRIAN ALDISS

Cretan Teat

This novel is entirely a work of fiction.
The names, characters and incidents portrayed in it are
the work of the author's imagination. Any resemblance to
actual persons, living or dead, events or localities is
entirely coincidental.

The Friday Project
An imprint of HarperCollins*Publishers*
77–85 Fulham Palace Road,
Hammersmith, London W6 8JB

www.harpercollins.co.uk

This paperback edition 2014
1

First published by House of Stratus,
an imprint of House of Stratus Ltd, Yorskhire.
a division of Random House, Inc., New York
House of Stratus 2001

A catalogue record for this book is
available from the British Library

ISBN: 9780007482214

Find out more about HarperCollins and the environment at
www.harpercollins.co.uk/green

Introduction

Yes, I went to Crete. And I came back.

How exciting was everything involved with *Cretan Teat*. If you happen to ask yourself why so few copies of this gorgeous novel have sold, well, read on. We shall come to that in a minute.

It was a new century and I decided to take Charlotte, my youngest daughter, with me to south Crete, in the mistaken belief that we could swim in the warm seas off the coast. But, simply plunging our naked feet into the tide was sufficient to disabuse us of that illusion. The Eastern Mediterranean had a message for us: 'Stay out!'

We went and had a drink instead, and studied our learning curve. The island was alive with such curves. We found that Crete had suffered a chequered history ever since the collapse of Constantinople. It had been prosperous under Greece, but was now – as was also the case with my daughter and me – a touch run down.

One day, I wandered through a forest of ancient trees, evidently designed by Arthur Rackham. There I found myself lost and came upon a small chapel, I felt, long ago abandoned by the family who had built it. I managed to get inside. In fresco on the wall was the portrait of a woman feeding what was evidently an infant Christ. The woman looked old and bore a halo. Not Mary, mother of Jesus. Back in the town, I sought out the village priest for information. (Ah, the thirst for information! The fuel driving a writer's engine!) The priest was sitting on a chair in his garden. He said we could not go inside; his wife was repainting the whole house from top to bottom. This either pleased or irritated him; it was hard to tell. He told me that the woman in the fresco was Sveti

Anna, Christ's grandmother. Mary, being a virgin, he explained, had run out of milk.

On the seafront, facing the cold grey ocean, was a family coffee shop. The daughter there served coffee to customers. When not thus engaged, she sat at a tiny desk behind the glass door, studying and painting in a Byzantine manner. I gave her a photo I had taken of St Anna, asking her to copy it in the Byzantine style. She said she could do it in a week – at which time, Charlotte and I would be gone.

I paid the young lady on the spot and received the painting when back in Oxford, it was to be the cover for the novel already brewing in my mind. You see, we trusted each other. The lady now lives happily in Athens, skilfully painting fakes for tourists in the Byzantine fashion. It seems that this story of St Anna is little known in the West. Her coffin lies in the East, in Hagia Sophia, in Istanbul.

A branch of the story I found myself likely to tell, lay beyond religion, in the grey alleyways and streets of ancient Kyriotisa.

Here, Hitler's forces in World War Two had invaded the town. Mothers and their children had been shut into the church and the church set on fire.

Here was a terrible story that had become wedged into the minds of the following generation, a story that was the antithesis of the Anna mother-care tale. Wherever one went, into garages, or food shops, or restaurants, or simple bars, there would be someone bleak of face to tell you about German war crimes.

I grew weary of their old song. I found myself asking: 'after the war, did not Konrad Adenauer himself come to apologise for Nazi atrocities? Why, German workers arrived and rebuilt the church and mended the roads …' And the waiter or waitress or whoever it was would ask scornfully, 'Why do you defend such villains?'

So there I was with my two sides of a story. What I wanted to add was something of the sexuality that happens when one is young – or not so young – and on holiday. Once we were home, I wrote my novel. A new company, Stratus, had just bought up fourteen of my past books; it seemed only civil to offer them my *Cretan Teat*. They accepted it.

So this is where we came in, as people used to say in cinemas running continuous programmes. The reason why this gorgeous and provocative novel sold so few copies, found so few readers, was because The House of Stratus in Old Burlington Street, London, was going bust.

My faithful editor at Stratus worked on, although she had been sacked. It was she who got it into book form complete with that cover and all. Meanwhile the 'Titanic' was fast going under. There was no distribution. Only the angry seas.

What you are now holding is virtually a new book …

Brian Aldiss
Oxford, 2014

'Where the bee sucks, there suck I ...'

Shakespeare, *The Tempest*

Chapter One

'What a bugger,' I said to myself, in my old-fashioned way.

'What an absolute bugger!'

There I stood, on a lump of mountain the name of which I did not know, in the sun, wearing a hat bought in the village. I was on holiday, wasn't I? Retired – almost – half-dead, youthful, solitary, moderately happy. Not a care in the world, you might say. In fact I was relishing the remoteness of this place, two miles down a lane, off a road leading nowhere very much, standing in a deserted olive grove.

There before me stood an undistinguished stone building, much resembling a cattle shed, with its front wall raised to form a peak above the roof denoting its function as a holy place. In this raised wall was an aperture in which hung a small bell – a bell which time had infiltrated, so that it could no longer move or give tongue. I stood before this venerable building mute myself, my adopted son Boris beside me. Our guide stood under an olive tree, smoking a cigarette, with no sense of the theatrical.

Completely dominating the chapel were the ancient olive trees, designed, to judge by appearances, by the artist Arthur Rackham. Over the centuries, their girth had thickened, they had grown gnarly arms and hands stretching out to detain visitors, while their seamed bark had created distorted countenances, like hostile anthropophagi with faces in their stomachs. Year by year they must be creeping up on the building, I thought. This little chapel was never locked, not once in its eight centuries of existence. I stood by it. My shadow was on its wall, together with the pattern of shadows cast by the nearer olive trees. All that was real, tangible. Even my shadow was tangible, in a manner of speaking.

And I had to go and get an idea for another novel. I stood there, while a story unwound in my head.

I had travelled several hundreds of miles to reach this particular olive grove, outside the village of Kyriotisa. I simply stood there and the idea arrived from… wherever it is ideas come from. What the relationship was between the reality of my situation and the unravelling proto-fiction in my head, I leave as a mystery.

This is one of the central questions, as far as I am concerned, the question of consciousness, and why to certain tormented minds do ideas present themselves unbidden, like gifts, which have to be pursued? All I wanted on this holiday was a blank mind.

Instead, I had this obsession with storytelling. And I would write about a man whose obsession ruined him.

The novel that sprang upon me would take at least a year's work, and then all that business with publishers, when really I wished to do nothing at all constructive. Maybe the odd screw here and there, if I was still capable of it, with some darling woman, and another helping of that amazing understanding men and women reach when locked together.

But it was a fruitful idea I had. I stood in the dappled shade, turning it over in my mind, while a lizard scuttled up an olive tree hand-carved by time. Its ancestors had probably lived in that tree in the days of the Paleologues.

'Are you okay, Pop?' Boris asked.

'Just thinking …'

The novel, I knew at once, would have two protagonists: a

contemporary man, a man of probity whose character would bring about his downfall, and a woman dead for two thousand years, whose legend was possibly false. He would be respectable, while she would be remembered only for her breasts.

Sex is not respectable. It is our last freedom, still untaxed.

Oh God, please not a novel with ideas. I can't cope with ideas; the racecourse is more my territory. I'm old, too old to be intellectual. I'm due for retirement, if not the funny farm. It's all I can do to hit the correct keys on my computer keyboard. When you are rapidly becoming impotent, a number of other inadequacies also kick into place.

However, if write another novel was what I was going to do, I had better get the starting point clear. I had better go back into the chapel and take a closer look at that painting.

The man who had led me to this particular olive grove, and this particular little chapel in the olive grove, reopened the chapel door for me. It was a low door, virtually a stable door. I'm a big chap. I had to bow low to enter. The threshold had probably been designed to induce humility.

The guide waited outside. He stood and smoked a cigarette.

Boris waited outside, ostentatiously patient. He dug his hands into his pockets and planted his right trainer on a stone, to stand there, leaning forward and whistling through his teeth. Boris had not acquired a taste for Crete's Byzantine mysteries.

The daylight died almost as soon as it crept inside the chapel. The candle I had lit still burned on the small altar, in a little haze of darkness. My passion for the mysteries and intricacies of Byzantium awoke again. Of all the pasts of the world, it was the most alluringly rich and religious and corrupt. Its music began to play in my head: deep, masculine, monotonous.

I stood in a small room, maybe three metres by four. A cattle shed, little more – probably built by men who understood only cattle sheds. Rush-bottomed chairs clustered there, vacantly waiting. Having gathered for a chat about old times, they had

3

found nothing to say. The chapel contained no ikonostasis; evidently the family who worshipped here were not the *créme de la créme*. Rather crude paintings adorned the wall, their holy images in blues and reds made indistinct through the erosion of neglect and the centuries. A smell of damp and aroma of candle, laced with the ghosts of incense.

This assemblage of reverend relics had remained imprisoned in this stone cell since the Paleologues ruled in Constantinople. A family of Kyriotisa had built the chapel, to worship here, generation by generation, until something untoward had happened. Wealth and prayer had failed them. Those remaining had gathered up their garments and had cleared off, perhaps to Hania to start a new life.

Without its congregation, their chapel had died, their olive trees had embraced the grotesque.

Modern me, I unholstered my Olympus camera, switching to flash. I focused on one particular painting, daubed on the irregular plaster.

The painting was of a woman nursing a child.

The woman's eyes had been scratched out. In consequence, her face was almost obliterated. Mould and damp had destroyed other parts of the painting. Age had mottled the plaster like a living hand. The head of the babe the woman held could hardly be distinguished. Not that the Byzantine artist had ever been numbered among the masters of his calling. Nor had he, poor man, enjoyed an intimate knowledge of a woman's anatomy. The breast the woman had produced for the babe's nourishment was the size and shape of an aubergine, and protruded from her lower rib.

Above the painting the wording was clear: *Agia Anna*. Saint Anna.

Shutter clicked, flash briefly lit, like the flash of inspiration. And again. And once more, from a slightly different angle. Better get it right, chum. You're not likely to come this way again.

Recollecting that time, as Boris and I walked back up the hill, I remember I was happy. It's a curious thing about happiness, that, unlike misery, it frequently eludes our awareness at the time; only later can we say, perforce using the past tense, 'I was happy then'. It is hard to determine if this is because for much of our lives we are experiencing frustration, disillusion, boredom, or even pain. We never get enough practice at recognising happiness when its wings brush our lives.

As Boris, the guide and I trudged up the stony way to the guide's car, we were shaded by gnarled olive trees, themselves witnesses to centuries past. The guide informed me that the saint's eyes had been scratched out by Turkish invaders. His tone was both confident and confidential. The eyes represented witnesses to the Christian church, which should not be allowed to gaze on the rituals of Islam.

I contradicted him. My argument was that the damage could have been more recent. It was too easy, in all lands which had been under Ottoman rule until after the turn of the century, to blame the Turks for everything. Maybe the Communists, or maybe the Nazis, who had occupied Crete in the early forties, had desecrated the image. Or what about the superstitious – those whose incipient blindness had moved them to scratch away the plaster of the saint's pupils, dissolve it in water, and drink it?

My faith in all these ideas was not strong, being unsupported by evidence; or maybe I had presented the guide with too many alternatives. He continued to insist the damage had been done by the Turks. The Turks were somehow to blame for the awful poverty that had recently befallen this entire area.

And why should I challenge his beliefs? He lived by them. It was his country. The man was not a fool. I was the fool. We both fell silent, contemplating, no doubt, my foolishness.

But I was the one with the photos, and the one with the idea for the novel. I was the one who was going to get rich – okay, rich by his standards… We walked companionably up the steeply winding track. Boris followed us. The day was hot. The afternoon was long.

We reached the guide's car, left by the side of the road. He drove us back into Kyriotisa. There we sat outside a taverna in the shade and drank a glass of retsina, from Hania, away over the mountains.

The first part of the story has to provide Archie Langstreet with a little background. Archie is a large, bullish man of mixed parentage. He has a big closed face, with a steep brow and craggy nose red from the Aegean sun. His square jaw and rather thin lips give him a look of determination. He is approaching retirement from his work with the World Health Organisation in Geneva. He is a decent, concerned, religious man, who takes his work seriously. Some of his colleagues would tell you that Langstreet is driven.

At present, he is holidaying on board a yacht hired from Pireus, with a hired captain. On board with him are his wife, Kathi, and a son by a former marriage, Clifford, together with two crew to cook and do all the donkey-work. At present, the yacht is moored in the harbour at Paleohora, on the south-west coast of the island of Crete. They have sailed around the island from east to west. Kathi, at least, is enjoying the respite from the tensions in Geneva, which are soon to come to a head.

That's enough background for now.

Langstreet sat in a beach chair, reading. A novel lay in the sand near his chair, but he studied a sheaf of papers, occasionally ticking a paragraph with an HB pencil. The pencil hovered, ever ready to peck at the legal document.

He paused, sighing. He gazed into the blue vacancy above the Libyan Sea. Through his sunglasses, the sky appeared a dark rich purple. Time passed. He willed it to pass. Sighing again, he resumed his study of the papers.

The beach was not particularly distinguished. It spread away

6

to the west, where a sea wall had been built; behind the wall was Paleohora's harbour, in which Langstreet's yacht was at present moored. Visitors ensured that the beach was moderately busy. Tourists lay on the sand, exposing various parts of their bodies to the sun, or sheltering under black-and-white rented umbrellas. Their naked bodies glistened with heavy oils, much like joints of meat roasting. Distant people shimmered like faulty ghosts in the rising heat. The margins of the sea contained infants cavorting and mothers guarding. The faint shrieks of the children reached Langstreet's ears.

From more distant stretches of water, a bikini-clad figure emerged, to come slowly up the beach to where Langstreet sat, shaded by wispy tamarisks.

'Oh, that was just brilliant, Archie! The water is gorgeous. You should have come in with me!' Kathi reached for her beach towel, to dry her face. Wrapping the towel about her shoulders, she stood dripping and looking down at her husband. 'I must have swum at least a mile. I don't have a fear of the sea any more, I just love it.'

'Don't get cold, Kathi,' he said, smiling up at her.

She put a chilly hand on his arm. 'Feel that!'

'You're like a frozen fish,' he said, with a short laugh. 'Better get dressed.'

'Dressed?! Don't you like me in my costume?' She struck an inviting pose, raising her arms and thrusting out her breasts. She was a dark woman, with honest grey eyes.

Langstreet set his legal document down carefully in the sand beside his chair, weighing it down with the neglected novel. 'Kathi, you are lovely, and we both know it. But I am in need of some action. You know I never was one for the beach. I'd like to see something of the island. Do you want to come with me for a drive?'

She gave a wail. 'Oh, Archie, you are indeed restless! We came here for you to take life a little easy – yet still you worry about this lousy law case... Where are you thinking of going?'

He told her he was planning to see what was happening inland, and asked where Cliff was. She told him to look across the road, with a certain edge to her tone.

Clifford could be seen sitting outside the restaurant of a white-stuccoed hotel, clad only in bathing trunks and a white hat, talking to a plump young blonde. His lean body inclined slightly towards the tanned female figure.

'Don't bother him, Archie. Let him chat up that Swedish chick. She looks nice. They are just being happy.'

Langstreet asked why she should imagine he was going to bother his son. He knew Cliff had to work fast, since they planned to sail eastwards on the morrow. Not that he greatly approved of such behaviour, but he recognised that the younger generation was freer in its sexual attitudes. Kathi, listening to this, bit her lower lip.

He gave his wife a frowning smile before turning towards the town, making off with his legal papers tucked under his arm. Kathi finished drying herself, applied Nivea Sun Lotion SPF 16 to her body, put on dark glasses, and settled down on her beach mat. She lay there crucified by the afternoon sun.

The little rent-a-car shop in the main street had a potted palm tree behind its plate glass front and only one car remaining for hire; a Fiat Punto, two years old. Langstreet took it. He considered the hire price absurdly cheap.

The engine sounded tuneful as he gradually accelerated. The outskirts of Paleohora fell away, giving place to olive groves in which goats roamed, followed by stands of bamboo. As the Fiat began to climb, these tokens of fertility died away. Soon he was driving among almost barren hillsides. Paleohora's isolation was written in rock.

No houses or villages clung to the winding kilometres. No traffic crawled along the road. No one walked here. Langstreet became bored. When he reached a lone village, sprouting ramshackle from the crotch of a steep bend, he did not consider it worth his stopping. After an hour, he drove into a small town lonely in the wild hillsides, which signs announced as Kyriotisa. Here he stopped. Consulting his map, he saw how Kyriotisa marked a geographical disposition. The way he had come was the descent towards the sea; the way ahead was the ascent towards Hania, the towns of the north Cretan coast and, at a greater distance, the great urgent world of Europe. Kyriotisa was where it was for good geological reasons.

He climbed from the car, and stretched. He was cramped and felt rather irritable.

It seemed as if Kyriotisa were having a nap, by way of celebrating the sun's passage from azimuth. A garage and service station stood at one end of the main street, to all appearances closed. The main street presented a dead, greyish appearance, although the shops were open. A dog crossed the road with infinite leisure. Billboards displayed rather faded advertisements for Coca Cola, brands of cigarettes, mobile phones, and Nentelstam Milk for Infants. On higher ground, behind the buildings lining the street, Langstreet could see the dome of an Orthodox church. Despite this token of higher authority, the town appeared to Langstreet to lie under a deadening materialism, the banal everyday. He took a turn up the street, observing that the town was built about a road that went in a great curve to avoid a severe drop into a valley. Behind Kyriotisa, hills rose almost immediately.

Entering a nearby taverna, he ordered a coffee, enquiring whether anyone spoke English who might lead him to old Byzantine churches in the district, as mentioned in his guide book. The waiter who served him with a cup and biscuit was a man with a grand moustache, his wrinkled face much resembling the bark of an old olive tree. He eyed Langstreet closely.

'You are Germany?' he asked.

'I'm English. Do you speak English?'

The waiter still looked dissatisfied. Raising a hand in a 'wait and see' gesture, he wandered into the street.

Langstreet drank his coffee, with pauses between sips. The taverna was completely deserted except for an old lady who sat in shadow, unmoving behind a counter.

The silence was broken when the waiter returned with a black-clad monk. The monk was corpulent, not particularly tall, his round weather-beaten face fringed by white stubble. Langstreet rose and gave him a slight bow.

'You speak English, sir?'

'You are from Germany?'

'No, I'm not. I'm from England, although I do in fact work in Germany. Germany and Switzerland. I am an official of WHO, the World Health Organisation. I am here on holiday. Why do you ask me that question?'

'The Germans were here many years and destroyed this place.'

'I can't help that. I'm English, as I've already told this waiter here.' Langstreet stood stiff and formal, looking slightly down on the monk.

'Then what can I do for you, sir?' The monk's expression relaxed as he asked the question. He moved a step nearer Langstreet's table, resting a hand on it, as though he found its weight a burden.

'I understand from my guide book that there are several old Byzantine churches hereabouts. I wonder if you could guide me to some of them? I have a car outside.'

'They are only very small churches, very old, very small,' said the monk with grave courtesy, as if he felt personally responsible for their shrinkage. 'They have no merit of architecture. Not a one can hardly be worth your visit.' When he saw that this statement made no great impression on Langstreet, the monk gestured to him to sit at the table again. He then took the chair on the opposite side of the table, saying, 'Yes, I will show to you some churches. We are glad to assist our English visitors. First you must know some facts about this place, Kyriotisa. Then you will understand more.'

He motioned to the waiter with a gesture of dismissal, speaking sharply in Greek, the results of which were that the waiter left, to

10

return some while later with two cups of coffee and two glasses of water on a tin tray.

The monk now clasped his heavy hands together on the table, hunched his upper body over them and began a long account. Most of the while, he stared down at the grain of the table, looking up sharply now and again to make sure that Langstreet was attending.

He claimed that Kyriotisa had once been a wealthy place. Its olive groves had made it rich. Its olive oil was regarded as the best in the Empire (by which Langstreet understood him to mean the Byzantine Empire). Its wealthier families were thereby enabled to build their own private churches in which to worship God. Often they built these churches in their own olive groves, the trees of which were sacred.

This was a happy period of calm and prosperity.

Worse times followed. Vendettas broke out among some families. Morality declined. Times were uncertain. A variety of rulers presided over the fate of trade. Also, there came a plague. The wealth all disappeared. The monk waved his chubby hands in dismissal of this vague period of history.

And then the war! Germans came and times were very bad, with many good people killed.

The monk looked up sharply at Langstreet. 'Many good people killed,' he repeated. 'A very cruel time.'

Time, Langstreet thought, when the arrival of another customer and the greetings this entailed brought a momentary pause in the monk's account, had somehow been squeezed from the narrative. The days of the Paleologues and the Venetians, the Ottomans and the Nazis, were all part of a seamless cloak of disaster. Only the uniforms changed.

According to the monk, the Nazis descended in strength on Kyriotisa by parachute.

'From the planes passing over they come.' He drew pictures in the air above his head with those same heavy hands.

11

The partisans fired on the invaders as they descended. The Germans exacted terrible retribution. People were shot indiscriminately, even children and women. The monk had been just a boy at the time. He had taken food up into the mountains to feed the partisans who lived up there. He remembered it well, going to the back door of the taverna, through the kitchen, to point to one of the mountains he'd had to climb.

He beckoned Langstreet to stand by him.

'There, you see? That one. I climb it once a week when I am young, with a loaf of bread underneath my shirt.'

His account of youthful heroism went on and on. The afternoon was growing late. Langstreet politely concealed his impatience.

As a reprisal for local resistance, the German soldiers had set fire to the houses of the village. Women, children and the sick had been sheltering inside the houses. All died. The fires could be seen up in the mountains where the partisans hid.

The partisans set a trap. They lured a German patrol to follow them into the mountains. The patrol was ambushed. The soldiers were made to jump, or were thrown, into a great cavity in the ground. Their cries were greeted with rejoicing by the partisans.

After three days, one of the local men was lowered on a rope to see if he could rescue some of the German weapons. The rope was old. It broke. The partisan fell on the bodies below. Some of the Germans were still alive, although their legs and heads were broken. They rose up and seized hold of the man. He shot them all.

The priest had many more tales of this sort. Langstreet felt sick and glanced at his watch, quickly, when the monk was gazing down at the table.

The Nazi commandant of the area had been a terrifying man. He rode about on a dapple stallion. He would execute locals arbitrarily, without trial. One day, a partisan sniper shot him. The partisans then wrote to Nazi HQ, explaining that they had shot the commandant because he was extremely evil and cruel, and that they hoped there would be no reprisals. The HQ had evidently formed the same opinion of their commandant: no reprisals followed his death.

Langstreet was finally moved to speak. 'This was all a long while ago, of course. Half a century. Things are very different now.'

'Not here!' The monk grasped Langstreet's wrist. 'Kyriotisa does not forget,' he said. He picked up the story again. 'After the war, in the early sixties, the Germans they come back again. This time, a very different crowd of them. This time, they wear suits, not uniforms.' He laughed, revealing his old yellowed teeth. 'To make up for what they do, they rebuild on a more grand scale the houses they destroy in the war. They build a good main road, and build a bridge over the river. They also build the large war memorial down the street, denouncing Nazi atrocities and listing the heroic dead among our partisans.'

At this point, the monk went into an exact description of the war memorial. He said that the inscription carved in the stone concerned the complete destruction of the town, which the Nazis had inflicted as a reprisal for the death of a few German soldiers.

'In fact, the post-war Germans gave back to Kyriotisa more than they ever take away. A ceremony was held, with a band from Frankfurt, when they left. Not one inhabitant of Kyriotisa waved or clapped or cheered them. So the Germans were forced to leave in silence.'

Langstreet looked challengingly at the monk. 'So, no gratitude from Kyriotisa, then? After an unrivalled and generous act of restitution? Why was that, do you think?'

The monk made a face, spreading his hands in dismissal.

'You must not think us to be unkind people. They did not gave us back our dead, did they? Or our lost limbs? Good riddance to them, I say.'

Langstreet stood up. He gave a slight bow, looking grim. 'Thank you for the coffee. I shall return to Paleohora immediately and not come back to Kyriotisa, thank you.'

'What's the matter? You don't wish to see the little chapels? Do you wish to see the war memorial?'

'I hate all this talk of war. It was over half a century ago, wasn't it?'

'Not for us, no. My father they shoot him in the back. My brother remains injured and is half-mad. I myself had to carry bread up that mountain in fear of –'

'Yes, yes, you told me about that. I'm sorry for you.'

The monk gave a sly smile. 'Sorry, eh? Well, you didn't do it. I just show you one little chapel. Quite near here. Don't be upset. You're British, aren't you? The British helped us in the war.'

While he was speaking, the monk was edging through the door into the street, holding Langstreet's sleeve with one hand while gesticulating towards his car with the other.

Telling himself to be calm, to see what he had come to see, Langstreet unlocked the car door and let the monk settle himself in the front passenger seat. He started the engine.

This passage seems to reveal something of the trauma existing in the town, as well as something of Archie Langstreet's character, without labouring the point too greatly. It is a tenet of his morality to believe that when forgiveness is sought, it should be given. Now I have to get him to see the painting of Agia Anna, where his response will be very different from mine. He is not a shallow man, not like me.

After Boris and I had seen Agia Anna, we travelled by bus back to our hotel, where we had a drink together. To be honest, we had a titter at the thought of the Virgin Mary running out of milk. After which, I hastened up to my room to have a shower, followed by plenty of talcum powder. At my age, there's always a suspicion that you may smell unpleasant.

I made a note about a possible story. It unfolded as I wrote. My main preoccupation was to meet up again with Ingrid that evening. Ingrid was a Danish lady of uncertain age, staying in the hotel with her daughter, Lisa. The daughter, a woman in her late thirties, was recovering from some kind of nervous breakdown. My sights, however, were set upon the mother, the amusing and civilised Ingrid Gustaffsdotter.

How was it that I sensed no sexual interest in the younger woman, and plenty in her mother? I suspected this inherited detection system – a cunning mixture of pheromones and body language, for a start – must have developed many generations earlier in human history.

Boris cleared off into town, disappearing with his usual brand of glum cheer. I settled down to wait in a comfortable wicker chair for Ingrid's return from the beach. I read a page or two of the novel I had brought on holiday with me. The novel, as if it matters to you, was by Arturo Perez-Reverte, entitled *The Victor Hugo Club*.

Ingrid and I had met at a nightclub the previous evening. A rather sly little friendship had developed. I loved her perfect English, spoken with that alluring accent. While I did not particularly wish Boris to know of this liaison, Ingrid seemed determined to keep it a secret from Lisa. Some recent incident, of which Ingrid would not speak, had upset this eldest daughter of hers. She also had two younger daughters in Denmark. They were safe in the care of an aunt. It was Lisa who most required her mother's protection.

Ingrid showed up at about four-thirty, immaculate in a pale green linen suit, with a wide-brimmed white linen hat. She wore sandals; her toenails were painted green. I put my novel aside and ordered us a bottle of wine.

We had a sophisticated way of courting each other, she and I; for Ingrid was a professor of English Literature at Copenhagen University.

So it was, over our glasses of Chardonnay, I quoted to her:

> Cupid's an infernal God and underground
> With Pluto dwells, where gold and fire abound:
> Men to such gods their sacrificing coals
> Did not in altars lay, but pits and holes.

She was quick to respond, from that same naughty Donne:

> Rich nature hath in women wisely made
> Two purses, and their mouths aversely laid:
> They then, which to the lower tribute owe,
> That way which that exchequer looks must go.

Such exchanges caused a stirring below the little wrought iron tabletop. As we talked, I became convinced that this lady, with her pink gums and pearly teeth, was deserving of what a lady novelist of my acquaintance genteelly calls, 'a kiss between the legs'.

As we were growing cosier in our conversation, seeing Lisa approaching, Ingrid said hastily, 'Climb over my balcony tonight – I'll be in my room waiting for you. I must take care that Lisa does not know of this.'

It can be imagined with what a fever I lurked in my room later that evening. I took a shower to cleanse and cool myself. I put on shirt and trousers. Ah, my dainty dirty-minded Danish dove, I may be getting on in years, but I am inventive and know more than one way to please you and surprise you. How are you feeling now? What do you hope for? What do you expect? It is entirely ready for you.

My room was next to Lisa's; then came Ingrid's room. Our rooms looked out on the Libyan Sea. Each had a balcony. Since the rooms were not large, the balconies almost touched each other; there was no danger involved in climbing from one to the next. I had only to cross Lisa's to reach Ingrid's.

Some minutes after eleven-thirty, I judged Lisa to be asleep. High with expectation, I went onto my balcony. The sea glittered under a moon shining high behind the hotel. What a night for love! Ingrid was old and soft and affectionate. I could imagine no greater bliss than to lie in her embrace! I went to the iron railing. I lifted my leg to swing it over.

Unfortunately, my damned leg was too stiff to reach the required level. I wrenched at the stupid thing. A bone creaked. It would not go. The first inkling of cramp warned me to cease my useless efforts.

I stood there in the shadows, out of breath.

How maddening to be thwarted by one's own limb! I had forgotten it was seventy years old. Even the independent-minded member nearby was more loyal to its master…

The furniture of the balcony consisted of a metal table and two metal chairs. As quietly as I could, I drew up one of the chairs, setting its back against the balcony rail. I climbed on to it.

The chair tipped.

I fell back. The chair toppled sideways with a clatter. With an even louder clatter, the table I struck with my shoulder capsized. I could hear the noise of it rushing down the street and out to sea, to alarm the fishermen at their nets.

Immediately, a light came on in Lisa's room.

Fatally injured though I was, I crawled away into my room, dragging my legs behind me, concealing myself just as Lisa came rushing out on her balcony.

Lying mute on the floor, clutching my knee, I heard her call her mother. Ingrid arrived on her balcony and the two exclaimed in Danish. By the tone of Ingrid's voice, I could tell she was soothing her daughter: 'Not a burglar, dear, merely a cat…'

Eventually, they both went back to their beds.

Eventually, I crawled into my bed. Well, there, I am seventy. What do you expect? Sometimes, ideas of romance outlive the anatomy.

Sprawled on the bed in total darkness, I found cause to reflect – as everyone must do at some time or another – that life, which seems so full of opportunities, denies us too much, whatever we do or refrain from doing, or find ourselves incapable of doing.

Perhaps this is one of the reasons why we enjoy reading novels: there, in the secrecy of their pages, we find persons who defy life and do those things – grand, awful, delectable, or trivial – which we have denied ourselves, or have been denied. You don't imagine that in a fiction I would have been unable to negotiate a balcony or two, do you?

It was when lying in bed that I began again to think about Agia Anna. It was curious to reflect that a rather vital episode in the life of the infant Jesus Christ seemed to have been edited out of the Gospels. Perhaps that censorship had been accomplished by prudes and religious bigots. There may be those who fear the female breast, as they fear the vagina, because of the lascivious thoughts they engender. Something of that nature may have accounted also for the flabby modesty of Agia Anna's breast, as depicted in the mural.

I could not help smiling at such reflections. Alas, I lacked seriousness. How different it was for my hero, Archie Langstreet. How much more Archie was destined to achieve than I!

Chapter Two

The monk in Langstreet's car directed Langstreet into wild and deserted countryside. At a certain bend in the road, the Punto had to be abandoned. Langstreet and the monk proceeded on foot. They made their way down a narrow track, which ran between ancient olive trees; the branches of the trees on one side of the way met the branches of the trees on the other side. It was dark here; evening was approaching. Langstreet stumbled on a stone.

'Who owns this lane?' he asked his guide.

'Fighting was all here,' said the monk, with a sweeping gesture.

'I asked you who owned the lane.'

'Maybe is Family Paskateris. At the end of the twelfth century, Byzantine noblemen moved to Crete. They fight against the Venetians. Once was very rich, long ago but not now. Except one man, is now our mayor.'

They trudged on as the gloom intensified.

At last, the monk grunted and stopped. He heaved at a section of fencing that guarded the grove on their left. It fell away. Langstreet climbed through, to stand amid rank grass. The monk followed, replacing the fencing behind him.

He gestured ahead. 'Here is a chapel, but is too near to darkness to see in a good way.'

They tramped among the trees, distorted into bizarre shapes by the extremes of old age. The gloom was pierced by a lingering ray of the setting sun which cut through a gap in the mountains nearby. Its smouldering light lit the front of a small stone building. The building was low and square, resembling a stable except for a bell set in its front facade.

The monk pushed at the door. It yielded grudgingly at his third heave. They entered with bowed shoulders.

A scent of incense, just a ghost of a trace of incense, reached Langstreet's nostrils. Incense, mingled with damp and age and old stories. The monk shone a small pocket torch.

'No, wait!' The thin white beam destroyed the atmosphere. Langstreet went to the rear of the chapel. There was only a cubby-hole, no ikonostasis: clearly this family, Family Paskateris, had not been of the wealthiest. In the cubby-hole lay a few brown candles, slender as willow twigs, and a rather damp box of matches. Getting a match to strike, Langstreet lit the wick of a candle. Its frail glow warmed the preoccupied lines of his face, making of it an ikon in the surrounding gloom. He carried the candle back to where the monk stood.

'Would you permit me to remain here alone for a moment, please?' he asked.

'I shall remain outside.' As the monk opened the door, Langstreet had a glimpse of the thicket of olive trees, hieroglyphics of age as they slipped into darkness. The door shut. He was alone in the old chapel. He crossed himself.

No windows punctuated the rough stone walls of the building. Four cane-bottomed chairs huddled together in a corner, refugees from family congregations. There came to Langstreet's mind the thought of his family's fortunes, his parents arriving in England, a foreign land, his mother dying – that pain, still attendant on him – his father's remarriage into a wealthy Scottish family, his own marriage to Kathi. That change of nationality a generation ago: it was brought about by the tides of history. This chapel must have represented security, piety, to a family facing the changing fortunes of time.

Langstreet was moved to kneel on a damp patch of carpet. Clasping his hands together, he uttered a short prayer.

'Great Lord, I thank you that I have been able to emerge from the darkness of an evil history into the light of goodness, through your good guidance. Here in this humble place where you still dwell, I beseech you to remain with me while I endeavour still to make restitution for the past. And I pray that my dear wife may come to understand these things which I do in your name. Amen.'

Whoever the generations had been, worshipping here, they had certainly experienced no diminution in the desire of the outside world for olive oil. But slowly their means of processing and distribution had fallen behind the technological advances elsewhere. Now the olive-crushing machines in Kyriotisa – those old-fashioned engines Langstreet had briefly glimpsed in the town – supplied their oil to Italy, where it was bottled and sold as genuine Italian oil. There was no longer a name for the Kyriotisan olive oil which once had been praised in Constantinople.

Shading the candlelight from his eyes, Langstreet rose to his feet and gazed about him. He felt the brooding presence of God. The door had no lock on it. Thieves were unknown. But there was nothing worth stealing.

The light shone on the rough-hewn stone walls, some of which had been plastered. Here, an artist-monk of long ago had attempted some religious decoration. Perhaps at about the time the Fourth Crusade was wreaking havoc in Constantinople, a monk had set out on the journey to Christian Crete, glad enough to escape the chaos in his city. It was apparent at a glance that he had been a poor artist, perhaps the best the Paskaterises could afford. Nor were the rough walls conducive to fine art. However passable the results had been when fresh, the centuries had been about their slow work in destroying colour and form.

One painting in particular claimed Langstreet's attention. It was formally headed *Agia Anna* and showed a woman suckling an infant. He took the candle closer, sheltering its flame with his hand.

The woman, St Anna, had had her eyes scratched out, the vandalism obliterating most of her face. The ugly child she was clutching sucked at a teat resembling an aubergine. It protruded from St Anna's garments somewhere about the lower rib cage. It was clear that the artist, holy man that he must have been, had scant personal knowledge of a woman's anatomy.

After gazing at the painting with reverence, Langstreet called in the monk, to ask him who St Anna was.

'Anna is auntie of Jesus. The Blessed Virgin Mary, she dries up her milk, so she gives Baby Jesus to his auntie for suckle. Here you see him at the breast.'

'The aunt of Jesus? I don't understand. What is the evidence on which this painting is based? It seems sacrilegious. It's not in the Gospels.'

'No, no. Not in Gospels at all. You find him in *Protovangelium* of James. In Constantinople was erected a church dedicated to Anna by Emperor Justinian. Is getting dark, sir.'

'Well, that's very interesting.' Langstreet placed a thousand drachma note in the cubby-hole, extinguished the candle, and followed the monk out into the open. Staring down at his boots, he said, 'I find it wonderful. A revelation.'

The monk closed the door firmly. 'Only one more such painting exists in all the world, sir. They tell it is in Romania or Bulgaria, or thereabouts.'

Once they were in the car, the monk said, 'I am only poor man, with no education. So I must live in Kyriotisa for all my life. You must speak to the priest for more better information, sir.'

'Thank you. You have been very helpful to me. Perhaps I may be permitted to buy you a bottle of wine when we get back to Kyriotisa.'

The monk waved a hand with nicotine-stained fingers in a

rough but courteous gesture. 'Sir, is not necessary. I am glad to help you, as British helped us in the war.'

Langstreet drove the Punto back across the mountains to Paleohora. The road twisted and turned as it sought a way to the sea. He encountered no other traffic on the way. At one point, he drew into the side of the road, climbed out and walked a short distance to sample the loneliness. Stars shone overhead. The moon had yet to rise. This place was unaltered from earliest times; he stood as if on a shore marking the boundary between bygone and modern worlds.

The sky overhead still retained some light, whereas the gloom of night had already settled over the land, emphasising its antiquity. In the distance, a line of land had been raised to resemble a giant hip, teasing Langstreet's fancy into imagining that he had trespassed on the sleeping body of some ancient being. He had stepped momentarily back from the ages of a Christian God into a time where women gave gods suck.

Hunching his shoulders, he walked briskly back to the car and the present day. He slammed the Punto door. Accelerating at once, he headed for the isolated lights of Paleohora.

Going down to breakfast next morning, I did my best not to limp. Out on the balcony, at the far table, smoking over a cup of coffee, sat Ingrid. She was alone, looking spruce and calm. I recalled that her daughter did not eat breakfast.

She gave me her usual smile, cynical yet warm, acknowledging, accepting, the follies of the world.

'Were you disturbed by the burglar in the night?'

'I thought I heard something.'

'I guess it frightened you off coming to see me.'

'Crete is known to be a violent country.'

'And England not so?'

'We're just a little country with a big language.'

'You should visit Denmark. We're a little country with a big hospitality.'

'I should like to enjoy your big hospitality, Ingrid.'

'Let me give you my address. Lisa and I must leave this morning.'

'I'll come and visit you, if I may.'

'I hope your leg will be better then.'

After breakfast, I sat in my room and began to write notes for my novel, until Boris came and suggested that we swam. When I returned to the foyer, I found that Ingrid and her daughter had already left.

Well, it was not important – just a mild flirtation, in which much or little had been said. That seemed to be about all I was capable of these days. What do you expect?

Nevertheless, I found myself dwelling with some tenderness on her features: the narrow temples and mild almond eyes, with the cheeks broadening out to accommodate a generous mouth. And her hair, dyed no doubt, swept back in good fashion, leaving a wing of fine quality over each ear. Inevitably, I then slipped into speculating on other parts of her body, of the snug exchequer tucked between her thighs, warm and resilient, ready for tenancy. But, alas, it was farewell to Planet Genitalia, at least for a while.

I could not help seeing myself as Dr Johnson's Rasselas, whose 'chief amusement was to picture to himself that world which he had never seen; to place himself in various conditions: to be entangled in imaginary difficulties, and to be engaged in wild adventures…'

For eleven years I had lived with an actress; a lady calling herself Diana Coventry, real name Doreen Stephens. Not particularly successful on the boards or even in TV commercials, but a pleasant woman, given to all those highs and lows with which the legendary leading actresses are assailed. In the dark, Diana might have been Vivien Leigh.

Doreen was as interested in the male sexual organ as I in the female. We never tired of looking as well as doing. There are men

I know, men heterosexual to a fault, who admit to disliking the look and aroma of a woman's genitals. I am not one of them.

I have a memory from early boyhood. I was in a cinema in Manila. A documentary was showing which employed a method of stop-motion photography on plants. From a bud of a flower, the sepals curled back and the whole flower slowly opened. Its interior revealed intricate details, while the petals, brightly coloured, unfurled, lined with marks to guide the bees to the honey at the heart of the blossom.

It was beautiful. For the first time in my life, I experienced an erection, entirely spontaneously. I was puzzled by the tiny disturbance in my shorts. From then on, I associated a flower-like beauty with the female organ.

Unfortunately, Doreen's and my years together were to end rather unexpectedly. I have always regretted our parting and, looking back, wonder if she has not later regretted it too.

Doreen secured a role in a soap. She played Viv Baker, a woman who ran a clothes shop in the West End. It upset our comfortable arrangements. She became the part. And when Viv Baker was required to indulge in amorous activities with the local crooked landlord, played by Larry Wingate, my Diana became more interested in Wingate than in me. Before I knew what was what, a note was on the fridge door, pinned there by a magnetic model of a London double-decker bus, saying *Adios!* (in so few words); and Diana was away to the suburb of Wimbledon with Wingate.

And so I was free to stew in my own juice. I have been rather at a loss ever since. Rather too prone to attend the racecourse.

It must have been nostalgia that prompted me at that point to pick up the phone, dial international, and try to speak to Doreen again.

A choked voice said, 'Yes, who is it?'

'Doreen, is that you?'

'This is Diana Coventry here. What do you want? I'm about to put the phone down.'

'Hang on, Doreen. It's me, your lost love, remember? I'm in Crete. I was just ringing to see how you were.'

'I'm utterly miserable, if you must know. Not that it's any of your business.'

'Are you missing me?'

'What makes you think that? I've just heard that poor Jav has died.' Jav was her brother. I had admired him. Jav was all that I was not: a man with good causes ever close to his heart, perennially adopting African tribes or giving starving Albanians holidays on the Costa Brava, or smuggling imbecile babies out of Romania into Finland. His eccentric ways had not endeared him to his semi-famous sister. When I had last had word of them, they were quarrelling bitterly. He was trying to borrow money from Doreen – all right, Diana – to fly pregnant leopards from the war zone in East Timor to a zoo in Australia. Darwin, if I remember right.

'I'm sorry. What did he die of?'

'I was just having a good weep when you interrupted me.'

'How did he die?'

'Alone. He had taken up the cause of some aborigines near Alice Springs. Just think, a brother of mine to go and die in Australia.'

'I don't suppose he could help it.'

'But Australia… How degrading!' Sob. Sob.

'It sounds romantic to me.' I was trying to cheer her up – always my role where women were concerned. 'Just imagine the abbo funeral. Didgeridoos wailing across the burning outback, dancing, fire, wallabies roasting on a spit, liquor consumed, screams, mass fornication… An ideal way of being sent off – better than a bloody church service…'

'Oh, you're so cruel, you wretch!'

Her phone clicked off. I remembered she was a bit on the religious side. I could but chuckle.

I had been contemplating writing a novel about my life with Diana Coventry when the better idea of Saint Anna came along. Well, I thought it was better. I sent an outline of the story to my agent, old Welling-Jones. True, there was the annoyance of this idea intruding itself upon a lazy Cretan package holiday, but one is fortunate when an idea arrives at all, no matter how inconveniently.

Kathi was sitting by the stern of the yacht when Archie Langstreet returned, wearing a new pair of blue velvet slacks and a white T-shirt without inscription. She had her evening glass of vodka and lime by her right hip. Every now and again she glanced at a portable TV set, by her naked feet, where two men and a woman were clinging to the face of a mountain in a howling gale.

She greeted Langstreet warmly and switched off the set. He kissed her cheek.

'Have you eaten, darling?' she asked.

'No, no. Where's Cliff?'

'Where do you think?'

'I don't know. Where is he?'

'You ought to eat something. He's with his Scandish blonde, isn't he?'

Langstreet grunted. 'Kathi, I've made an amazing find. A crude painting of the infant Jesus being suckled, not by the Virgin Mary, but by his aunt. I came across it in a chapel up in the hills. Eight centuries old. Part of the Christian legend the Christians appear to have forgotten.'

She laughed, switching off the television set. 'A bit of blasphemy? A schism within the holy ranks?'

'I'm given to understand that it's a neglected part of holy legend. Certainly the family who owned the chapel believed in Anna and reverenced her.'

'Oh, there can't be a jot of truth in it, surely. It's like Max Ernst's famous painting of the BVM giving young Jesus a good walloping!'

He sat down on the deck beside her, being careful to place a newspaper underneath him to protect the white of his canvas trousers.

'The story can be authenticated. That I mean to do. You must take this seriously, Kathi, my dear. If it is true, it is very touching. It seems that, according to my guide, the Virgin Mary's milk ran dry, so auntie took over.'

She sat there frowning, drawing her knees up to her chest.

'Does the guide believe this to be true?'

'He doesn't know much about it. He claims there is only one other such painting in the world – apparently in Bulgaria or Romania.'

Kathi chuckled. 'Can you see her tits?'

'One breast protrudes. It's very modest.'

Laughing, she said, 'Pity you didn't come across a painting of the Virgin Mary showing her tits!'

He wagged a finger at her. 'That would never be permitted. It's no laughing matter. You're being indecent. I must speak to a local priest and find out more about the subject. The painting is clearly something of a rarity, and should be preserved. There it is, rotting in a stone shack in an olive grove.'

She remained silent for a while, or else was listening to the lap of water against the sides of the boat.

'It's an ikon, is it?'

'No. An ikon would most likely have been stolen long ago. It's a wall painting or a fresco.'

She said slowly, 'An ikon would have been better. You could have used it, couldn't you? I mean, against bloody Nentelstam.'

Archie Langstreet and his wife were taking a vacation while his lawyers in Geneva sought to amass the final sheaf of documents in a legal battle of long-standing. As a senior official in the WHO, Langstreet had been assigned to see the case through. His official title was Director of ACDW (Against Commercialisation of the Developing World). The case was due to come to court in November, after three years' work. Nentelstam had done everything in its power to delay and muddle the issue. Langstreet was dedicated to concluding the case, and winning it, before his retirement.

Nentelstam was well known for selling its formula powdered milk to mothers in the Third World. That breast-feeding obviated the danger of many diseases and the risks of becoming pregnant again was considered by the powerful international company to be none of their business. If Langstreet hated anyone, it was the faceless Nentelstam corporation, with its ruthless drive to open up more markets.

New scientific evidence had recently come to light, fortifying his case against the corporation.

He told his wife now that no ikon was going to make Nentelstam change its mind or its policies.

'But an ikon of Jesus being breast-fed,' Kathi urged.

'There's no ikon, my dear.'

'So you said. But wouldn't it be a powerful persuader for your cause? "Breast-feeding could turn your son into a Saviour…"' She sketched the sentence in the evening sky with a finger. 'Don't you see, Archie? If there were an ikon, it could be reproduced all over the world.'

'It's a good idea, Kathi. Brilliant, now I come to think of it. But – *if* there were an ikon… Only there's not.'

'If there were an ikon – '

'*If* there were an ikon?' He regarded her grimly, not smiling.

She stood up. 'We'll go shopping in the morning.'

Cliff was up early next day. The sound of his singing in the shower woke Kathi. She slept naked. Drawing a silk robe about her, she went on deck to survey the scene. Distantly, two fishing boats had drawn in, and there were men working at the nets. The boats were painted light blue, with eyes under the raised prows. Otherwise, the harbour was deserted. The sky was overcast with light mackerel cloud. A breeze toyed with her light brown hair. She inhaled deeply before going below to brew coffee and wake her husband.

After breakfast, Cliff went off to find his new love. Langstreet and his wife went ashore to find a priest. Of the people they saw,

29

the tourists wandered as if lost, whereas the locals were more purposeful, though unhurried. Gaining the main street, they asked a waiter in the nearest coffee shop where a priest might be found. The waiter obligingly walked with them for a hundred metres before pointing up a side street and giving them directions.

They walked up a street lined by mutilated trees. Taking a turn to the right, they entered among ranks of smaller houses, most of them decked with flowers. The last house in the line, standing in a small garden in which honeysuckle flowered, was the one described by the waiter as the priest's house. It was in no way distinguishable from its neighbour. Kathi rang the doorbell.

They waited.

'Shall I ring again?'

'He may be out.'

'Doing good?!'

'Doing no harm, we hope.'

The door opened. The priest emerged, to stand there blinking benevolently at them, turning a blue-streaked rag over in his hands. He wore the customary black robes of the orthodox priest, and the customary round black hat. His face was wrinkled, its rich brown colouration setting off his white beard. He pursed his lips and raised his dark eyebrows in mute question.

'We need your advice, sir,' said Langstreet. 'Do you speak English?'

'What nationality have you?' enquired the holy man, narrowing his eyes to scrutinise Langstreet. 'English? German?'

'We're English,' Kathi told him. 'We have a religious question to ask you, if we may.'

He gestured largely, and began to walk slowly towards the garden at the side of the house. As they followed, he said, 'You see, I decorate my house. I have some paint. Therefore I cannot ask you inside it. We shall sit in my garden. There you can speak.'

The side garden was untidily bright with pink and blue flowers, among which courgettes and peppers grew. In the garden, sheltered

30

by vines, stood a ramshackle table and chairs. The faded blue cushions on the seats of the chairs had once borne a pattern, now all but obliterated by wear and weather. The priest gestured to them to sit down. He seated himself after they had done so. A small bell hung from a chain by his right hand. This he shook once or twice. It gave off musical notes. A small bird in a wooden cage nearby echoed the sound.

The priest asked courteously how he could assist them.

'In the hills above Kyriotisa, I came across a painting in an old chapel which interests me greatly. It portrays the infant Christ being suckled by his aunt Anna,' Langstreet began.

The priest raised his hand immediately. 'Pardon. Agia Anna is not the aunt of Jesus Christ. She is his grannie.'

Kathi snorted with concealed laughter. 'His grannie? On which side of the family?'

The priest, without relaxing his good-humoured expression, said, 'Is not that rather a silly question, madam?'

Langstreet interposed hurriedly, saying that a monk had told him Anna was the aunt of Jesus.

'The monks are poor men. They are good but they are countrymen, you understand. They have not much learning. Only a few scriptures by heart. They sometimes lack even Biblical knowledge.'

Langstreet remarked that he did not recall the legend of Anna giving the infant Jesus suck in the Bible.

'You must look in the *Protovangelium* of James, in the second century. There it is clear. Grannie, no aunt. Saint Anna. Mother of the Blessed Virgin Mary. Her relics are preserved in a chapel in Rome, as I recall.'

'Well, that makes that clear,' said Kathi, regarding her husband with merriment in her eyes. Langstreet evaded her glance.

A sturdy old lady, with an apron over her black, ankle-length dress, appeared around the rear corner of the house, carrying a tray. She smiled graciously at her husband's guests and set down the tray before them. Her brief journey had disturbed the arrangement of some biscuits on a patterned plate. She set them into a star pattern, smiling absently as she did so. With gestures of invitation, she then retreated.

Cups of coffee and small cakes lay before them, beside the biscuits in their neat pattern. The priest, whispering a word of grace, invited them to help themselves.

'So this grannie still had breast milk when her daughter had run dry?' Kathi said.

'Such is the report of James,' the holy man said. He then looked enquiringly at Langstreet, who asked why this legend was not better known.

'Is no a legend, but history. Wait, I have it in a history book, which I will fetch. Please enjoy your coffee.' He rose and disappeared around the corner of the house. Kathi chose a small cake, while Langstreet selected a biscuit.

'Jesus' grannie!' Kathi exclaimed in a whisper. 'Ask him if there's an ikon. There must be!'

The priest returned, leafing industriously through a heavy volume bound in black leather. He had put on a pair of rickety spectacles and, having seated himself again, he stared at the pages through which he leafed, muttering to himself.

Finally, raising a finger, he looked up.

'Here we have the details. This is an English *History of Byzantium*. I bought it during my stay at Oxford, some period of time before. It has been written by Doctor George Layton. Listen!'

He proceeded to read.

'Mmm… "Two centuries and a half had almost passed away. The Byzantine Empire had been destroyed by the Crusaders – " that is the Fourth Crusade, of course' – and the Asiatic Greeks were endeavouring to expel the piratical Genoese from Crete. The Emperor Michael Paleologos was besieging Constantinople without success. Some Greek officers, wandering through the ruins of the church and monastery of the Sacred Family, admired the magnificence of the edifice, despite its ruinous condition. They could but lament that so splendid a monument to Byzantine piety should have been converted into a stable under the ruinous administration of the Ottoman conquerors.

' "In a corner of the building, a remarkable tomb which had recently been desecrated arrested their attention. Within the sarcophagus lay a well-preserved body of a woman, richly dressed. An inscription upon the broken lid of the tomb proclaimed these to be the mortal remains of Saint Anna, mother of the Blessed Virgin.

' "Later, the Emperor Michael VI visited the spot. He ordered that the body be preserved and removed to the Monastery of Our Saviour, since when it has been lost to human cognisance." '

'No ikons were made of Saint Anna?' Langstreet asked.

'Justinian erected a church in her honour.'

'But no ikons?'

The priest shook his head. 'Why are you on this quest, sir? What happens to be your interest?'

'I am a connoisseur of ikons, and am keen to acquire one of St Anna.'

'I cannot help you there. Maybe there is no such ikon.' His strong white teeth bit into one of the cakes.

'Thank you for your help, sir.' Langstreet extracted his business card from his wallet and handed it ceremoniously to the priest.

The quiet town of Paleohora exhibited signs of life when tourists, returning from the beaches, sought a midday meal. Still Langstreet's hired yacht lay moored on the quayside of the main harbour. Along the eastern beach, where shops and tavernas grew more modest, stood a shop selling ethnic wares, including a number of ikons. Langstreet and his wife entered the crowded little room, to be greeted by numerous representations of the good and bearded.

A corpulent woman of middle age emerged from behind a

counter at the rear and asked them if they would like to buy some local silverware. She clasped her hands before her, over a worn brown dress.

Langstreet was inspecting the ikons. All were modern reproductions, and garishly coloured.

He asked the woman where her ikons came from. She told him they were manufactured in Athens, at a workshop in the Plaka, a centre for tourist activities.

'But a real ikon painter? Are there any in Crete?'

'Not a real painter, no.' She nodded her head, before adding, 'But is old monk who does such things. He lives in the gorge.'

'What gorge is that?' Kathi asked. 'The Samaria Gorge?'

'No, no. I show you.' She retreated to the rear of the shop, and they followed meekly behind her broad back.

The woman fished up a biro and a paper bag from under her counter. On the bag she drew a rough line to indicate the south coast of the island. Marking the position of Paleohora with a cross, she drew a ragged line to the east of it, from the coast inland.

'Here is Gorge Mesovrahi.' As she drew another cross halfway up the gorge, she said, 'Here is Church of Agios Ioannis. Here you will find the Monaché Kostas. He will show his ikons. Is very old.' She handed the bag to Kathi.

'Can we get there by road?'

'Is no road. Only by sea you get there.'

Langstreet and his wife exchanged glances. He asked the woman, 'Are you sure this Kostas is still alive? There's a village, is there?'

'No village. Is church. Kostas is still living. I know it. He is my relation. His name is now Christodoulas – "He who serves Christ".'

Thanking the woman, clutching the paper bag, they left the shop. It meant sailing back the way they had come, and so probably returning the *Southern Warrior* late to the rental firm in Piraeus.

'Why not? It sounds amusing,' said Langstreet. The remark was an uncharacteristic one, as her glance at him indicated.

'And maybe something more than that.'

They sat in a taverna with Cliff, drinking frappé and consulting a nautical map. The mouth of the Mesovrahi Gorge was only some nine nautical miles from Paleohora, an easy sail. Cliff said he did not wish to come.

'Oh, come on, darling, it'll be a bit of an adventure.'

He smiled at her. 'I'm having my adventure here, Kathi. If you're away overnight, I can stay with Vibe… Yes, in her hotel room… Oh, don't look so old-fashioned, father! The hotel won't care. You can pick me up when you come back.'

'Do come with us, Cliff,' his father said. 'You should not sleep with a woman so easily. Besides which, it's safer if we're together.'

'Safer?' He shook his head with affected weariness. 'What danger is there here?'

Langstreet shrugged. 'You never know.'

So far so good. I get the impression that Archie Langstreet is a decent, serious man. Quite a different character from me. Perhaps there is an echo of my son in Cliff. On second thoughts, no, not really.

I have said very little about Boris. I call him my son, but he is not a blood relation. At one time I was living with a decent woman called Polly Pointer. My life was then sane and orderly.

Polly was superintendent of a home for unwanted children, and that was where she picked up Boris. His parents had beaten and abandoned him. She brought him home one day, a small sad mite of a boy who said nothing for two or three weeks. Tell me I have no sense of responsibility, but Boris was not popular with me.

Polly and I quarrelled over the boy. I said she should have consulted me before bringing him home. The bad feeling between us was not improved by the child's filthy habits, which were slow to improve.

Not that bad feelings got in the way of our fascination for each other. Here was a woman who accepted responsibility, who cared for a number of people with horrible habits. And Polly did care – in

35

a calm, deep way. What did she see in me? I was an independent spirit; I did not have to answer to a board, as she did. Also, at that time I was immensely popular and successful. I appeared frequently on TV chat shows. I was on the Literature Panel of the Arts Council, dishing out money to those less fortunate than myself (you notice that the money has run out, just when I'm broke). My novel, *Whom the Gods Hate*, was short-listed for the Booker Prize. All this success faded when Polly died.

There was more truth than I had bargained for in my epigram, adopted from the Greek, 'Whom the gods hate, they first make famous'.

It seems as if, looking back, I was earning enough money to iron out our differences and live and love in some style.

As circumstances eased, Boris improved. Polly was applying to have him officially adopted. Then the home where she worked rang one day to say that Polly was injured. I left the lad with a neighbour and drove to the hospital in Bournemouth where she lay.

She had been run over in the driveway of the home. A client making an angry retreat had hit her as she ran to pick up a child who had fallen over. She died two days later, without regaining consciousness.

After the funeral, I was stunned by grief. Only then did I fully realise what a good woman she was, and how much I loved her. And how I had often quarrelled with her unnecessarily.

Poor dear Polly! I had taken her for granted. What do you expect? That's life, as they say. She had been so joyous; without that joy, I was one of the walking dead.

For Polly's sake I did not get rid of Boris. He was by now a lonely and still oddly behaved little boy. I tried to talk to him about Polly.

'She didn't love me,' he said. He was merely responding to the pattern of his life.

'Yes she did, she loved you very much. Polly chose you of all the children in the home.'

'She didn't love me, or else why did she die?'

How often I cried over that very question; it was one I could not help asking myself. How self-centred I was, crying more for myself than for her.

Now I think of it, I remember ringing my literary agent at that time, about something or other, and telling him that only women were capable of real joy. Not men. Men hid their incapacity in obsessions, such as writing. Real joy was granted only to women.

'And how do you make that out?' he had asked.

'It's a fact, Will. Something everyone knows. Like the fact that if you live in London you're never more than a yard from a rat. Men should be humble before women, and serve them.'

'Jesus,' he said, and put the phone down. I then recalled what a big woman his wife was.

Anyhow, to cheer up this narrative a bit, I must relate that I bought Boris some livestock to keep him happy. I was such an inadequate father. Firstly, I bought him a pair of ring-doves. Boris would be quiet in the garden, sitting on a log, to watch those pretty birds for hours, as they were cooing and flitting from tree to ground, strutting, flirting, seemingly everything to each other, the most contented of creatures.

For his indoor companion, I bought him an iguana. We went together to a pet shop and chose a small common iguana, young but wise-looking. Years later, Fred, as we called him, had grown to be five feet long and became rather a problem; but Boris and I loved him from the start.

We got two goats, which were rather a nuisance. But why am I telling you all this? So that you will know something of this rather silent lad, now almost a man, who still lives with me, who came on holiday with me to Paleohora, and remains a mystery to me, as I to him. He is studying to be a naturalist. His affections are directed, not to women or men, as far as I can see, but to the world of birds and animals.

Much of my present trouble springs from my flying Boris to

Tuscany to celebrate his sixteenth birthday. Our intention was to take a party of four friends, two adults and a girl and a boy, with us; but one of them fell ill at the last moment. Boris and I went alone, to a large, sparsely-furnished house in the wilds. I had a book to write. Boris cycled about the countryside, watching for wildlife.

One evening, as I sat on the balcony with a glass of wine by my elbow, I saw Boris coming along the valley road, pushing his bike. With him was a young woman, walking in a confident manner. A woman, or girl, I should say, he had met in a village trattoria. This was Lucia, a pretty dark-haired girl, whose breasts were noticeable under her T-shirt. She wore shorts and mountain boots. They were excited, since Boris had captured a rare butterfly in a specimen jar, so introductions were perfunctory.

I was disturbed. Somehow, that sight of Boris and the young girl, with the bike, walking along that road among the poplars, seemed oddly familiar and consequently disconcerting.

'I'll cook us some supper,' I said.

I poured them some wine before going to cook. Lucia – little more than a kid – followed me into the kitchen. Boris tailed after her.

Lucia said, lifting up the jar containing the butterfly, 'Boris must let this poor creature go free, don't you think?'

When I agreed with her, she flashed me a smile. Just to keep in practice, she took to flashing me enticing looks. I told myself they meant nothing. I like women, am generally on good terms with them, but these young specimens of their sex, just come to puberty – heaven preserve me from them!

Boris was eager to please Lucia. He emanated, he seemed to be surrounded by, a blush of emotion. Until this time, I had not seen him exhibit any sexual desire. Certainly, Lucia seemed as pleasing a cause of desire as any girl could be, if you were young and rash enough, and had a lot to learn. Old though I was, I was shortly to find I too had much to learn.

The sun had just set behind the hills. We stood outside as he opened the specimen jar. Out flew the butterfly. As it fluttered to the corner of the house, a bird flew swiftly past, snatching the insect in its beak and making off without pause. It was a terrible moment of synchronicity.

Over the meal, I asked Lucia if she was staying the night.

'I think I will. Soon I will become a film star.'

This curious conjunction of sentences needed some thinking about. I hardly listened to Boris' explanation of Lucia's fortunate meeting with a British film crew making a mystery-thriller set partly in Florence. Boris seemed to my eyes clumsy and unsophisticated when compared with this sparkling and confident young creature.

'Will your parents mind?' I asked.

She looked at me as if I had come from the Ark. In reply, she gave what novelists call 'a tinkling laugh'.

After the meal, Lucia started to make up to Boris, becoming coquettish and teasing him, after the manner of her kind. He was embarrassed in front of his father, so I left the house and walked through a fine night, down to the river. There I listened to the swift flow of water over the pebbles on its bed. That ceaseless energy made music through the darkness. Admittedly, I felt some envy of my son, having such a pretty girl in tow.

My heart ached for my lovely Polly.

Stars came out overhead. I watched them through the trees and thought about my life, and its unsatisfactory quality, which I recognised as being mainly of my own making.

When I returned, the youngsters had gone up to Boris' bedroom at the top of the house. I went to my room and slept. The room was stuffy. I slept naked.

A shriek awoke me, followed by a male cry. Grabbing a towel with which to cover myself, I rushed up the stairs to see what was happening. Perhaps our isolated position had invited criminals to invade us.

A light burned by the bedside. Boris lay in bed, his back turned to the light. Lucia, naked, stood on the bed, kicking him in the ribs.

She turned to me. 'The bastard oaf! As soon as he is in me, he has his bloody orgasm and is done for! I kick him, of course!'

She gave him another kick. I ran and caught hold of her legs. 'Lucia, please! He's miserable enough! This is no way – '

But she fell over, and I with her. She locked her arms round my neck and kissed me forcefully. 'You are a real man! You must lick me, lick my poor pussy now! I need it so much. I am sex-crazed.'

She spread her legs to show me what was in store for me. The English sense of shame to which we seem born played no part in her make-up, then or when I encountered her later. What I saw was received on my senses as irresistibly beautiful.

Well, without requiring further invitation, I did as she bid, and more. It was as if I had gone blind to the rest of the world, including my son, who dragged the duvet around himself and crept from the room, sobbing as he went. What do you expect?

After her first orgasm, when I was out of my senses with lust, I brought my little soldier into action. In those days, he was punctual in coming to attention, and not – as happened later – inclined to beat a retreat without firing a shot. With my left hand, I held her head so that our mouths were together, while my right hand slid down between those luxurious buttocks. I positioned my middle finger as a sentry in her bumhole, so that no heat could escape. In this way, I had her nooks and crannies well covered.

Delight? There's no word for it!

For days afterwards I went about glowing in the ambiance of those timeless minutes. But the little sweetie took off. I barely had time to discover that she wore hold-up stockings with pretty bands of lace at the top (when she was dressing, I mean) before she was gone – leaving, or rather taking away, a large hole in my life.

I was never one to resist a pretty crutch. She was delectable in every part. Nor did I imagine that Sylvia Beltrau – as Lucia later became known – would mutate into a famous film actress. But that lay in the future. Right then, there were only her textures, her tastes, her squeaks of delight to remember.

In Paleohora, three years later, Boris still surrounded himself in gloom. The failure seemed permanently to have affected him. He came with me as one who had nothing better to do. My feeling was that he could not forgive me. He barely laughed at the idea of Christ being suckled by his grannie. I was ashamed of his suffering.

When I met Rosemary, I was suffering from a bout of diarrhoea.

But I had better get on with the story.

Chapter Three

Langstreet's boat, the *Southern Warrior*, rocked at its moorings. The water had an uneasy swell on it and was dark. Cloud overhead was streaky and active, wind pulling long streamers of white and grey across the sky. Kathi cast a weather eye up-wards and pulled a face, saying nothing. Langstreet talked to the captain.

'Is okay. Will blow over soon. No problem,' said the captain. They had heard that before. It was generally true.

The water at the quayside was uneasy and splashed against the hull as they boarded the boat. Langstreet was dressed in vaguely nautical fashion, with a navy-blue parka over a T-shirt. Kathi wore a powder-blue trouser suit. He held her hand to assist her on board.

The captain started the engine with a jerk. Once out on the open sea, the waves became considerable; round the head, the wind blew with force. Kathi clung to the rail, enjoying the gusts which buffeted her face. The clouds grew thicker, darker.

After an hour, with the weather getting heavier, Langstreet urged the captain to stay further out from the coast, since there was a danger they might be driven onto the rocks. The captain replied that they were in no danger. 'No problem,' he said. 'Is okay.'

As Langstreet retired, a sudden squall hit the *Southern Warrior*.

He slipped, lost his footing, went down, and crashed into the forward hatch. The hatch struck him in the back. He cried out, but Kathi was already coming to help.

'Confound these shoes,' he said. 'I've broken my back…'

She held him, wedged against the wheelhouse. She was afraid to move, kneeling protectively over his body.

The captain took this accident as a signal to steer the boat into a moderately sheltered creek. As he moored the boat, rain began to fall, slashing down in torrents, drowning the small world of the craft with its noise.

Kathi called to the captain. 'Help me get my husband below deck.'

The captain stared at her and frowned. 'I'm only paid to sail the boat, not act as a stretcher bearer.'

'What are you saying?' She could not believe she had heard right. 'Help me get my husband below. He's badly hurt.'

'I'm not to blame for his carelessness, am I?' the man replied. He came grudgingly forward. She had hardly made any close observation of him before. Now she saw how brutish he was, with the rain running down his face. His nose was broad and broken. Beneath his reddish moustache his mouth was open as he panted with exertion, revealing broken teeth. But he took most of the weight of Langstreet as they manoeuvred him down the short companionway.

Once they were alone, and the flimsy doors closed against the storm, she made Langstreet comfortable on his bunk. Kathi strove to get him out of his sodden clothes, pulling off his T-shirt and trousers. By now, Langstreet was protesting he was fine. She then pulled off her own flimsy garments, and snatched a small towel to dry herself with.

'That looks good. Come aboard,' he said, eyeing her body, and the drops of water glittering in the fleece of her mons Veneris.

She was startled to be invited. Sexually, he was not a forthcoming man. She saw, however, that he was beginning to be excited; his

43

penis moved against his leg. She climbed carefully over him, kneeling with one leg on either side of his body, her breasts stirring as she did so.

'You're sure you're up to this, Archie?' she asked.

'Try me.'

She was nervous in case the captain came in. When she inserted Archie's penis into her vagina, she said, 'Just a quickie for you, darling.' She then commenced leisurely but firm movements on him.

She did not have to work too long.

And the captain did not intrude.

The storm lasted for some hours – hammering at the cliffs which loomed above the boat, raining ochre tears – before fading abruptly. It was getting towards sunset when they set sail again, on a sea shedding its grey looks for a more youthful blue-green. Kathi was relieved to find that her husband had suffered nothing more than badly bruised ribs. She bound him tightly with bandages from the First Aid cabinet. Langstreet made no complaint about his injuries. He merely offered thanks that no bones had been broken. Possibly his anger at the captain served as a distraction.

He gave the man a good cursing, which the captain took with scowling brow, muttering that he was being paid only for sailing the ship, and poorly paid at that.

As dusk was setting, they came into the mouth of the Mesovrahi Gorge, where they moored at a small jetty. The cook prepared a modest meal, which they ate on deck as the sun sank in a splendour suggesting that all previous sunsets had been merely dress rehearsals for this particular one. They split a bottle of retsina between them.

During the night, both Langstreet and his wife had terrible dreams. Archie Langstreet dreamed he was a crablike creature of metal, living in the core of the Moon like a grub in an apple. It seemed he had bought the Moon. When he crawled from his den into the open, it was to find that the Moon was lying on its side, abandoned on a stony beach to which there was no visible end. The land was barren. A sea of purple sent in against the stones, waves carved of lead, slow, heavy, despairing.

Kathi Langstreet dreamed she was walking down a strange street. The shops on either side were locked. People stared through windows at her. At last she came to a place which was open. It was a café. Above the doors was a sign saying, 'Futures Café'. She entered. A man said to her, 'Sorry, the chairs are on fire. Don't put your *something*' – when she woke she could not recall what he had said – 'on one.' She did not notice any flames. Only when she ordered a glass of water did she realise that the whole place was burning down about her. She woke in a fright, to lie there listening to the creak of the boat.

The dawn was newly hatched, making the sea gold, as if yolk had been spilled from a gigantic egg. Suiting the simile, the smell of bacon frying tickled Langstreet's nose as he rose, showered and shaved. His ribs ached, but his temper was good.

After the meal, he and his wife prepared to make their way up the gorge, the mouth of which was as yet in misty shadow, giving it the insubstantial air of a Turner watercolour.

Langstreet instructed the surly captain to wait until they returned, whereupon he and Kathi set forth to find the Monaché Kostas, the old ikon painter.

A stream coursing from the mouth of the gorge spread over the pebble beach. Both husband and wife were wearing trainers on their feet. They paddled into the ravine mouth, between tall cliffs topped with ragged edges, the wide open jaws of the gorge. A weatherworn kiosk, a tooth in the jaw, stood to one side, closed and shuttered in decay.

For some hundred metres the way ran almost horizontally, although studded with boulders, which needed to be circum-navigated. Then the gradient started. The gorge was wide here.

Nevertheless, they walked one in front of the other, with Kathi bringing up the rear.

Langstreet muttered something.

She asked him what he had said.

Without turning round, he repeated, 'The Nentelstam Corporation.'

She knew how his mind ran on the protracted legal case against the corporation, so made no response. The sun climbed over the shoulders of the gorge and shone down on them as they made the slow climb. At one point, the gorge widened where the cliffs had crumbled. The remains of an old building stood here. Langstreet leant against the walls of the ruin and panted.

'Let's have a break.'

A small spring burst from the cliff behind the ruin. Kathi went over, cupped her hand beneath the flow and drank. She splashed water over her face.

'It's good, Archie. Try some. Are your ribs hurting you?'

'Slightly.'

When he had drunk, she thought he said, 'Long train sat here at a fat-arse seat.' The cliffs distorted his voice.

'What train?'

'Thinking aloud.' He turned to face her, panting. 'I'm talking about long chain polyunsaturated fatty acids. In the breast milk Jesus drank. You know… They help to nourish intelligence. You don't get LCPUFAs in Nentelstam's infant formula… So the infants are less intelligent than they might have been if raised on the female teat. Heavens, it's hot…'

She scrutinised him, seeing how unwell he looked. The skin of his face was blotched. He spoke with increasing incoherence. Gazing up at the long quim of sky overhead, he muttered, 'Boring Mediterranean sky. No clouds for interest. Got to get home.'

'Archie, you're ill. Go back to the *Warrior*, or you're going to collapse. I shan't be able to carry you.'

He looked at her despairingly. 'Maybe I'd better. You come too.'

But she had decided to go on. It could not be much farther to the church of Agios Ioannis, where the Monaché Kostas lived. She would pay him to paint an ikon of Christ being suckled by the Virgin Mary's mother.

'Can you do it?' Langstreet asked.

'Sometimes I could kill you,' she replied.

He gave her a weak smile and, without a word, turned back the way they had come.

Once she was alone, Kathi struck up a better pace. The heat intensified. She walked on the shaded side. The gorge narrowed until she could touch either wall with her arms outstretched. She waded through a coursing stream. The sweat trickled off her, through her clothes, between her thighs. The cliffs on either side trapped the day's heat and, more oppressively, her thoughts. Who it could be at her side she did not know, yet she addressed it.

This companion seemed to wear a hat and have no eyes.

Archie has such problems. This lawsuit preys on his mind. And then he will have to retire. He doesn't know what he'll do with his time. I don't know... There's a sort of, what? A settled sullenness about him. No lightness. He makes enemies. I see it in their eyes, not liking him.

I can't make out what he thinks of me. Perhaps I don't figure very large in his scheme of things. Whatever his scheme of things is. Well, I know really. I think I do. He wants to be a great man. He wants to be acknowledged as someone great. Someone who's made their impact on the world. What a terrible weakness. It ruins his life. He was born too rich. The money spoilt him. Maybe that's my trouble too. Spoilt. Selfish. Somehow he's got to justify himself. A great man! It's awful...

And the thing walking with her said, in a gobbling kind of way, through its dirty sandy mouth, 'It's halfway to madness. It makes you more unhappy than you know.'

No, but I care about him.

47

'Oh no, you don't,' it said in a dark, chuckling voice. 'You never really cared.'

That's so unfair. I do care about him. I like his body, for instance.

'Thoughts suppressed breed cancer, heh heh heh. You'd better watch out!'

'Piss off, you wretch!' She aimed a blow at the figure and struck her hand against the wall of rock. Nobody was there.

Nursing her bleeding hand, Kathi slogged on.

The gorge had run like the slash of a giant sabre into the land. Now it became wider, shallower, less taxing. Kathi had walked for an hour. She leaned against the rock, alternately clutching her bleeding hand and wiping the sweat from her face. When she had recovered somewhat, she surveyed the scene. The walls of the gorge were lower here. The impression was that she was in a valley. Clustered on one side were houses, little more than huts, which appeared deserted. Nearby stood a modest building, built of stone. From its elevated façade a bell hung. It was the church of Agios Ioannis.

A goat was tethered in the shade of a small tree. A bench and a table stood near the church. On the table were a bottle and a tumbler. In the tumbler some wine remained. Kathi went and sat down on the bench. She rested her head on her folded arms. Her world went into a spasm of crimsons and greens, dotted with pinpoints of light.

'You are fatigued, lady,' said a compassionate voice. 'Vous est fatiguée. Sie haben Ermordung.'

She replied without looking up. 'No, *Ermordung* means murder. You mean *Ermuedung*. That's fatigue.'

In an altered tone, the voice said, 'So you are German lady, yes?'

She sat up wearily. 'I'm English. I speak German. Who are you, exactly?'

The man standing beside her wore the traditional black habit of Orthodox priesthood, complete with black headgear. He was small and wizened, an orange long past its sell-by date. His mouth was almost hidden behind a thick white beard, his eyes by thick eyebrows – two snakes peering from bushes. His ears luxuriated in dusty furze.

A group of people had gathered behind the monk. They remained at a distance in Attic poses, two stalwart women, an old bent man leaning on a stick, a child holding on to a corner of its mother's apron.

'You are unwell? Come with me to the monastery. I will give you lemonade.'

'Thank you. And you are?'

But the monk was already heading for the house nearest to the church. He walked with a decided limp. The choric group made way for him. The women stared with curiosity at Kathi as she followed.

The room into which they entered was as stuffed with objects as an over-furnished dolls' house. There was scarcely room to move between a narrow bed and an old table. The table was cluttered with the remains of a meal, or perhaps of several meals. A platter was partially eclipsed by a stack of manuscripts. There were also oil paints and a half-finished painting. One wall contained a small shrine where a paraffin light glowed. Another wall was covered almost to floor level with ikons of various sizes. A third wall specialised in electronic equipment – a hi-fi, a television set, a radio, a computer and a fax machine – from among which the face of Jesus looked out, calm and a little supercilious.

The monk indicated that Kathi should sit at the table. She removed a tube of vermilion and planted herself on a rush-bottomed chair.

'A moment!' he said. Opening a back door into what Kathi glimpsed was a kitchen, he shouted for a woman to come in.

'You have arrived from the sea coast?' he asked, perching himself on the edge of the bed. She swivelled to face him before answering affirmatively.

'You have no man?'

'He's not well. He returned to our boat.'

49

'He's invalid?'

'No.'

'You relations with him are good?' The snakes peered out of the bushes at her.

Irritated by this line of questioning, she stood up and gazed at the ikons hanging on the wall. Venerable faces of calm, bewhiskered sainthood stared out at her. The saints were dressed in angular garments, their folds sharply emphasised. They stood before a stylised portico of a church, or else in a vacuum of gold leaf. Most of the portraits exhibited such clarity, it was as if the holy men needed no obscuring air in which to breathe.

For Kathi, the religious import of the paintings meant nothing, the style of painting everything. There was here a conviction, a formality beyond anything in Western art, which drew from her a deep and disturbed response, a mingling of respect and rejection.

She replied to him as he had done, with another question. 'Are you the Monaché Kostas? I come with a commission from my husband.'

'Are your relations with him good?'

'They're as good as can be expected. We wish you to paint an ikon for us.'

'Excuse me. If your marriage is breaking, then I cannot paint an ikon, for who would pay me in such a case? You see my problem.'

A woman entered from the kitchen, bearing a tin tray on which were a pitcher and two glasses of minute size. She set the tray down precariously and poured lemonade into the two raki glasses.

Kathi took a glass and drained it at a gulp. 'More, please! I'm so thirsty.'

As more was being poured, Kostas the Monk said, 'Excuse me, when did you last have a sexual relation with your man?'

'That's none of your business! Shut up about it. I wish to commission an ikon. I will pay you a deposit in advance. We don't need this personal business.'

'But I see you are troubled in your relationship. I can give you spiritual help.'

'I don't want, I don't need, your spiritual help, thank you.' She grabbed the pitcher and poured herself another thimbleful of lemonade. The large woman, who had stood there stolidly, said something to Kostas with an air of disapproval.

'She asks if you have a bad thing in your past,' said the monk.

'For God's sake! That's none of her business either.'

'We must be friends if I am to paint for you, yes? Our histories are part of us.'

'Our bank accounts are more important than our personal histories, and in this case – '

But the monk had risen to his feet. Stretching wide his arms, he proclaimed that he knew nothing of bank accounts. Bank accounts were ungodly. History was the important thing. History was all round us. History decided what a man should be.

'But – ' said Kathi.

No interjection would stop Kostas' oration. He was born many kilometres from Agios Ioannis, in a place unknown to his visitor, called Kyriotisa.

'I do know Kyriotisa, as a matter of fact,' his visitor said, but her contradiction was swept away on the tide of oratory.

In Kyriotisa, he continued, he lived happily with his family, who had their own small olive grove. Life was good. They had a goat and hens and a well of good water. As a boy, he fished in a lake and caught trout for their supper, for which he was much praised. Then German armies invaded Crete.

'Oh, for God's sake!' cried Kathi. 'Not the bloody war again! That was fifty years ago. It's all over, done with, gone.'

The monk gave a savage cry. Rolling up his cassock, he planted a foot on the table. He had a plastic leg, joined at the knee to real flesh. Kathi stared in horror at the pink plastic, and the stained straps securing it in place.

'War is not over! Is not gone! Is here still, in my leg!'

He went on to say that he was training to become a policeman when the Germans invaded. He had immediately taken up arms, and became a partisan in the hills. He spoke eloquently of the atrocities committed. Kyriotisa was burnt to the ground. The young woman to whom he was engaged had been raped by three Gestapo officers. They had cut off her breasts and bayoneted her.

This last remark was addressed, not to Kathi, but to the stout woman who stood by the table. She clutched the lemonade jug to her bosom, unmoved by a recital she had no doubt heard before.

'What did you do in return?' Kathi asked, coldly.

'We would not let them get from such atrocities.' He enumerated some of the devices of retribution, fixing Kathi with his little serpent eyes.

'Stop it! That's enough!' She felt she was in a madhouse. 'These terrible crimes – on both sides – they happened long ago. They should be forgotten by now.'

'My leg! My affianced! How do I forget them?' After the war, when the Germans had been driven out of Crete, law and order was re-established in the province of Canea. Kostas emerged from the hospital in Hania and returned to ruinous Kyriotisa. He was no longer able to train as a member of the police force. As he asked rhetorically, 'Who would wish to have a policeman with one leg?'

Kyriotisa echoed with mourning. He became a lame monk and studied the Holy Scriptures. His character became more and more solitary. He admired paintings of the Byzantine period. He began to copy them. Soon, he saved up enough money to buy paints. He copied many frescoes. What he particularly admired were the frozen attitudes of the saints.

Of course. They echoed his own frozen attitude to life, thought Kathi. (As an author, I am privy to my characters' thought processes.)

As his imitation of the rules and standards of the specialised manner of painting – 'heraldic', he called it – improved, his ikons were bought by a merchant, who displayed them in his little shop.

They sold to tourists, who were not fussy about whether a painting was genuine or fake. So he contributed a little to the return of prosperity to Kyriotisa.

One day, the Germans returned. This time, they wore civilian clothes and drove in big cars. They threatened to take over Kyriotisa and rebuild it. They had big smiles and gifts for the populace, but still they were the same Germans. The same Germans! He emphasised the point, smashing a clenched right fist into his left palm.

Kathi felt bound to contradict him. 'No. They were not the same. Nazi Germany was defeated and overthrown. I have heard this story before! This delegation from Bonn, from a democratic Germany, came to make amends for the destruction they had caused. Is that not the case?'

Spit issued from the monk's mouth as he cried, 'The case! The case! Madame, the people were scared from their wits! They did not hope ever to see another German. It happened that at that very moment, as the big cars drove up, I was hearing that a living became available here in the gorge, at the Church of Agia Ioannou. So I took it and left Kyriotisa forever. Here I live happily in meekness and suffering, loving everyone, hating nobody, serving the Good God in every way I can.'

'So perhaps you did not hear that the Germans made honourable amends. They rebuilt the houses which had been destroyed. They mended the roads. They constructed a bridge over the River Kyros. They even built a war memorial, commemorating the Cretan dead, and admitting to the Nazi ferocity. Can you imagine such genuine penitence, or such generosity ever before?' She felt her grasp on grammar faltering before the monk's broken eloquence.

He clenched his fists together by his chest.

'Pah, repentance! Nothing! They rebuilt the town so as to have a good plan of everything, the houses, the new hospital, the roads, so that they would know exactly where everything was the next time they invaded us. Why do you defend such villains?'

She saw it was time to keep quiet. To argue against such obsessions was useless.

'You were clever and fortunate to be able to build yourself a new life here, after the war. I have heard that your ikons are much appreciated.'

'No thanks to the Germans.'

'But German tourists buy them, don't they? These days, the Germans are entirely different. They too suffer from the Nazi past, and do their best to be good citizens of the world, you know.'

'But you are English?'

'I told you so. Now, Monaché Kostas, about this ikon I hope you will paint.'

She brought out photographs of the crude painting of Agia Anna that Langstreet had found in the little church amid the olive groves. Kostas knew nothing of the legend. He examined the photograph closely.

'Is a small breast for Jesus. Not like this woman here.' He indicated the woman who still stood by them, clutching the jug. 'Is for politeness and religion the painter paints a small breast. Maybe was really a big happy breast.'

He let his gaze linger on Kathi's shirt.

'How long will the work take you? We do need it rather quickly. How much will you charge?'

He shook his head. As he stood there, apparently thinking, she thought how much she hated him and his encasing xenophobia. It was a relief that Archie was not with her. The man's prejudices would have been more than he could bear.

'No money to pay yet. I do much research in colours and attitudes. Then I paint and varnish. If you don't like, then you don't pay.'

'How much, then? How long will it take?'

The old mouth opened in a dry laugh. 'Always the European question, no? 'How much?' 'How long?' Madame, I need time. Just some little time. Then I speak. Is a big difference between our nations – we have the time, you have the watches.'

The aphorism checked her. 'Say, ten thousand drachmas? Twenty? What size will you paint it?'

He clicked his tongue, protesting that as a poor monk he did not need too much money. Four thousand would be enough. He bent down and produced a piece of wood, measuring about 300 by 360 centimetres. He would paint on this block.

'It will be like these paintings on the wall? These are your work?'

He raised his head in the Greek gesture meaning yes. 'You see, I have the time to take care.'

She saw in his humility another aspect of the man. The man with a wound had shaped his life to become an artist. She told herself he needed respect rather than hatred.

'I would like to give you some money now. As a token of my sincerity.'

He contradicted her mildly, saying that money was only itself, never a token of sincerity.

'You will take a little meal with us, Madame. Then you must return to this husband of yours, to arrive before dark. What name has he?'

'Archie.'

Suddenly, he smiled, an old broken smile with something warming in it.

'Mm. Archway? Like a bridge between two different points.'

'If you like.' She turned to examine his ikons again, avoiding any more questions. The woman left the room. Kostas stood silent, gazing at the photograph of Agia Anna.

Finally, he said, almost to himself, 'It is possible, of course. In God's world, all is possible.'

In God's world... She felt vividly that this little man had recreated a fragment of God's world in his art. That it repeated slavishly the old formulae into the twentieth century lent it an extra attraction.

They ate in the shade, outside the back of the house, on two old rickety chairs. It was a dish of sliced tomato and goat's cheese, onto which olive oil had been liberally poured, served with a hunk of bread and a glass of retsina. She recalled a similar rustic setting in the heat, long ago. She had come upon it during a holiday on a Greek island, after she had taken her degree and had become a doctor. She had travelled with another girl. Sheila. They had met up with two Italian youths, also holidaying.

She had not greatly liked Umberto. The heat and their near nudity, and Umberto's importuning, had persuaded her to make love with him. It had not been as exciting as she had hoped for, but – she now remembered – she had been pleased afterwards to have had him do it. Such things were what one went on holiday for.

Why think of that occasion now? It meant nothing. Oh, but Umberto had sung to her while they swam together. She had enjoyed that. Archie never sang. Perhaps she had heatstroke. Yes, she had *Ermuedung*. The goat's cheese was good. Why should Kostas have offered her spiritual help?

After the meal, she thanked Kostas and started back down the trail through the gorge.

I will spare everyone, including myself, an account of Kathi's return journey down the gorge. These days, anyone can imagine what it's like to walk down a gorge. You can read about such things in the travel pages of your Sunday paper, or see people doing it on television.

I have never been down a gorge myself, though I did once see the mouth of the Mesovrahi from a cruise boat. No, that's untrue. A lie here is a real lie, whereas anything that happens in my story is neither true nor untrue in the same sense, since everyone understands it to be a fiction. Not that I intend a lie in the fiction; indeed, I make it as truthful as possible, within its own fictive realm. Though I recall Iris Murdoch telling me that in fiction one approaches truth through an ambush of lies.

Or perhaps, more poetically, she said 'an ambush of loves'.

To say that I suffered from diarrhoea in Greece is a statement of a different kind to saying that Archie Langstreet suffered from diarrhoea in the same place. You may choose to believe or not to believe in my attack (though I could take you to the actual toilet in the hotel in Piraeus where much of the attack occurred); but it would be idle to discuss whether or not Archie suffered from the same undignified upset. Rather like arguing about how many children had Lady Macbeth: how many craps did Archie Langstreet have?

Of course, some people are particularly interested in such things. One lady friend of mine noted that people pee a lot in my novels. Was this, she was implying, an obsession or an attempt at realism? Or was it my own bladder speaking?

Anyhow, there I was on the terrace of this hotel in Piraeus, surrounded by roses swarming up trellises, reading *The Victor Hugo Club*, and a bit bored, when I fell into conversation with Rosemary. This was after that disgraceful but delectable occasion with Lucia, mentioned earlier. I could see that Rosemary had a rather superior air about her. In fact, I found later that she was Lady Rosemary de Vere. She was contemplating divorcing her husband on grounds of cruelty.

So she told me, after we had downed a vodka or two, followed by a glass of retsina, while pecking at mezedes. Right there on the terrace. Contrary to what you may read in novels, it's pretty rare, at least in my experience, to be able to pick up a woman in a hotel – which you might consider to be a kind of social *Exchange & Mart* – however actively one remains alert to the possibility. It's a little discussed fact of life that most people travel in pairs, or are about to meet the other half of their pair, or else are trying to pick someone up themselves, or aren't worth picking up. But Rosie – it was Rosie by the time we ordered a light lunch together – Rosie and I were getting on well, and laughing a lot. Two delightful dimples, east and west of her lips, appeared when she giggled.

Then, over the deep-fried kalamari, came a terrible stabbing pain in my stomach. I was being polite, striving to give the appearance of a cultivated man, while she was telling me at length how amusing were the novels of Surtees, particularly *Mr Sponge's Sporting Tour*.

I sat there, pretending nonchalance, until my stomach growled audibly. With an excuse that it was time for my literary agent to phone me, I hastened upstairs to my room and the toilet.

It must have been the crab. I had eaten crab the previous evening at an outdoor taverna, having just returned from the islands. Why did I eat that crab? I had been uneasy about it, even while eating. Was it not sufficient for a brainy chap like me, that by merely removing the 'bee' and substituting one of those 'pees' this erstwhile lady friend of mine had believed formed a leitmotif in my work, I might have seen through the word 'crab' to what it really was?

As I crouched there, my stomach releasing itself downwards, I saw the notes I had left on the toilet floor during my last visit. Unlike my malady, the notes had some claim to being of intellectual moment.

'Is it conceivable that by careful arrangement of the twenty-six letters of the alphabet on paper I am able to account for my life, however passionately or dully lived? And that those letters can be reduced further to something on a silicon chip, expressed as noughts and ones? Am I merely an arrangement of such insignificant symbols?'

Although I had found it a painful reflection, I could not fit it into my current novel, even as ballast. So I jot it down here. A profound thought while evil gases fill the cubicle. Perhaps I am to die in my own crabby stink… Well, what do you expect?

So I return with feigned nonchalance and a change of underpants to the intriguing lady on the terrace, and my mixed fish dish with capers. A new but empty glass stands on the table; the intriguing lady has refreshed herself with another vodka while I have been away. While I can only respect this opportunism – which will go on my bill – I cannot but wonder if Rosie is on the verge of becoming an alcoholic.

I inform her that my agent has been offered an advance of ten thousand pounds for my new novel. Rosie smiles a gentle and beckoning smile. I find myself leaning towards her across the table, almost upsetting my glass of Chardonnay. And then the pain returns.

But she insists on telling me what she describes as 'a risky story'. She's well away. The dimples are deeper. Because of the pain in my stomach, I miss the preliminaries, and cannot determine whether Rosie is attempting to tell me a joke or is passing off her far-fetched story as a joke.

It seems that a cousin of hers, an Australian immigrant, lost an arm in a farm accident. In a beet-crushing process, his arm was caught in the machinery and had to be removed at the elbow. An emergency operation was performed.

In the same hospital ward lay a man who was brain-dead and was shortly going to be taken off the ventilator. The authorities came to a quick decision. They removed the arm of the brain-dead man and replaced it on the living cousin. It was an intricate operation. Nerves had to be connected, as well as veins and arteries, and bones reset. Five surgeons worked on the operation, which lasted for eight hours. At this information, my stomach gave an audible *ping!*

The operation was successful. It took a few weeks for the arm to ease into full working order. Rosie's cousin was delighted. Unfortunately, his new arm and hand took on a life of their own. They kept feeling up the cousin at embarrassing moments. Next, they took to masturbating him when he was asleep. A medical enquiry was conducted, in which it was disclosed that the offending limb had originally belonged to a homosexual.

Ultimately, the cousin became so enervated that he underwent a further operation, and had the appendage surgically removed.

Joining her laughter, feigning mine, I made an excuse and ran for my room.

While I was seated on the toilet, there came a knock at the door. Rosie called, 'Coo-ee! Can I come in and use your loo?'

Compared with my trivial affairs, the Langstreets had more important issues to face. Kathi eventually reached the mouth of the Mesovrahi Gorge. In her weariness, she knelt and bathed her face in the seawater. As she rose, her husband called angrily from the boat, 'Kathi, what on earth kept you so long? Come aboard at once!'

It was not the welcome she had expected.

She climbed wearily up the gangplank, retorting that she had done what Archie wished and commissioned the ikon.

'It's not important now,' he said. 'Kathi, we're in serious trouble. A police message has just come over on the radio. Cliff has been kidnapped.'

'Oh, no, I don't believe it. I must sit down.' She did so. Archie stood over her, sternly waiting for a better response. 'I need a mineral water, please, Archie. What's Cliff got himself into now?'

Her thunder had been stolen again. She knew that the ikon had been dear to her husband's heart; otherwise, he would never have allowed himself to be deflected from the pursuit of the Nentelstam Corporation. Now she had returned from her excursion, not to congratulations, but to find a worse thing had occurred.

Archie had calmed himself. He called to one of the crew for a bottle of mineral water. When it arrived, he poured his wife a sparkling glass full to the brim. As she sipped, he stroked her arm.

'The police report said Cliff was seized on the quayside. Three men jumped out of a van and forced him into the vehicle. This was after dark last night. Vibe, the Swedish girl, witnessed it. She was with Cliff. She screamed and shouted. No one came to help, and then the van was off... We must pray he is unharmed...'

'Is this – it's the war again, is it?'

He nodded, looking grim. 'Now you're back, we must return to Paleohora.' He started shouting instructions to the captain.

Kathi put a detaining hand on her husband's arm. 'How did they find out – about us – about you?'

He said, impatiently, 'How do I know? Maybe it was something Cliff said. These bastards – they never forget…' He turned from her and went to secure the gangplank. The captain cast off and in a moment they were away.

'Is Vibe all right?' she asked, into the breeze.

'Vibe? Yes, I suppose so…' He stared forward. 'It's Cliff I worry about.'

Once they were out of the bay, a freshening wind met them. The sea today was blue under a blue sky. The sun shone on the brisk wavelets. Langstreet and his wife stood in the stern, arms linked, saying nothing, but unable not to feel a little better in the spanking surroundings, with progress being made as they headed westwards along the coast.

'You're all right – bodily?' she asked, rubbing his back.

'Fine. No bones broken. And you? How was the monk-artist?'

She thought. 'They're so poor. That tends to give them long memories. Otherwise – no events. I mean, a life of poverty spells a life without pleasurable diversions such as we enjoy.'

He frowned at that, but she continued.

'For that reason, events such as occurred during the war stay present in the mind. Also, the old monk has a false leg to help keep them in mind. A curious thing Kostas said – talking of the West – "You have the watches, but we have the time". Maybe having the time isn't so good for you, if you're stuck in it.'

'Yes, poor fellows…' He spoke vaguely, his mind on other things. 'I assume they will not kill Cliff. This is their way of getting at me through him. Maybe they'll exchange me for him…'

'No, Archie! Please. Don't think it. Get in touch with the British Embassy, or whatever they have here. Pay them the ransom. Don't let them get you!'

He put a hand over his eyes. 'Oh God, you can never be free of it, can you? The past clings like mud. What have Cliff or I done to deserve this?'

They were silent. The cliffs peeled by to starboard. The boat sliced through the sea.

'I do pity them,' he said, his mind turned back to the invasion. 'It must have been a ghastly time... Airborne invasion...'

Kathi could think of no way to console him, except by wrapping her bare arm around his waist. He gave no sign. In a while, she went below to wash herself and change her clothes; after which she lay, tired and disconsolate, beached upon her bunk.

Sleep overcame her. She roused when the captain called that he had sighted the peninsula of Paleohora ahead.

Chapter Four

I read in today's *TLS*, the literary newspaper, a review of a new translation of the writings of Heinrich von Kleist. It mentions one of von Kleist's most striking essays, 'On the Gradual Production of Thoughts Whilst Speaking'. It is many years since I first read this essay, but I remain impressed by what I take to be its main contention, namely, that, during a conversation, one says things which one would never have thought to say when silent and alone. This is one of the benefits and pleasures of good conversation.

So that when at length I opened my hotel room door to Rosie de Vere, and she said, sniffing, 'What a nice smell of coffee!' I responded unpremeditatedly, 'The hotel does not provide a deodoriser in the toilets. So I quickly switched on the percolator to drown the stink. I'm sorry, Rosie, but I have an attack of diarrhoea.'

I had not intended to admit it. But, in obedience to von Kleist's rule, I suddenly decided to be honest with a nice woman who, as it turned out, was not ultimately going to be honest with me.

'My stomach is upset too,' she replied. And then she kissed me.

Externally, there was nothing wrong with her stomach – or, indeed, with the rest of her body. It was all a bit sudden but, in the excitement, I did not bother to ask myself why she was in such a hurry.

So there we were, the coffee percolating, and both of us naked on the bed, mouth to mouth, genitals to genitals: a very happy position. We began on our sides and then, as pressure mounted, I rolled on top of her. She had me in such a grip, suddenly tearing her lips away to gasp for breath, for her orgasmic breath.

The thought of what she was undergoing brought me on too. And in that bliss which reigns over the mindless short sharp strokes, I released something more than semen. An obscure muscle reflexed, and once more my stomach evacuated itself of the stuff that plagued it. It splashed down our conjoined bodies, brown lava on white flesh, thus fulfilling von Kleist's dictum that 'it is not we who know things but pre-eminently a certain condition of ours which knows'.

Rosie was remarkably forgiving. We showered together and called the housekeeper to restore the bed to its pristine condition.

Dining together that evening, she confided that she was to meet her sister, Claudia, and Claudia's little daughter, in two days' time. Perhaps I would like to join the party, if I was still in Piraeus? I hastily assured her I would remain in the hotel and would love to meet her sister; and thereby I sealed my own downfall.

I spent much of the following day alone in my room – Rosie had mysteriously disappeared – writing notes. A writer lives by notes. I wrote a little sketch of our love affair so far, taking care to make it more romantic by omitting any mention of stomach upsets. Already a plot for a light romance was forming in my mind. I could work Agia Anna into it somehow.

Suitable thoughts would flow in earnest once I embarked on the actual novel. A novel is, in von Kleistian terms, much like a conversation one has with oneself. Ideas are generated in a surprising way as one goes along; it is this pleasing experience that keeps one writing. For whom does one know as amusing as oneself?

On the morning of the day following, I was in my room, selecting the best clothes to wear when accompanying Rosie and Claudia, when the phone rang. It was Rosie.

Rosie had bad news to tell. She had just met Claudia and her child off the ferry from the neighbouring island of Aegina. Claudia was emotionally upset. Her husband had left her without warning for a young bimbo. Rosie had always said that Cyril was too wealthy to be decent. He owned Idaho Instruments. So Rosie was going to put her sister to bed in her room. Unfortunately, Claudia was also unwell and running a temperature. It looked like malaria, she said.

'What rotten luck!' I said. 'I didn't know you could catch malaria in the Med.'

'It only looks like malaria. Perhaps it's meningitis.'

'Where is Cyril now?'

'What does that matter?' Rosie asked, sharply. 'I'm in trouble, dear, and I need your help. Claudia's little girl is very sweet, but she's in the way. She can't play here, while her mummy's trying to sleep. Could you possibly be a darling and look after her for an hour or two?'

Silence. 'I'm not much good with children, Rosie, to be honest.'

'This one is properly behaved. You'll hardly notice her.'

I asked, 'How old is this child?'

'I'd really be most awfully grateful, darling. She's getting on for three – an angel. You could go over to Aegina on the ferry – she'd enjoy that – and play on the beach. Please, sweetie! Come to a poor lady-love's aid.'

'Well, I don't know…'

'Oh, thank you so much! You're a brick!'

Did she say *brick*?

And by eleven o'clock, I was on the ferry with Violet Herbage Potts. Certainly the child was well-mannered and docile. At first she said 'I want my daddy,' rather too frequently; understandable enough, if she had been told that daddy had run off with a young

65

bimbo. But a ride in a horse-and-carriage along Aegina front seemed to please her.

I bought her a spade and pail and a little bathing costume and paddling shoes. That also pleased her. We then took a taxi out of town to a beach called Marathonas. There I was able to sit in the shade of a tree and sip retsina, while the child larked about in an aimless way, in the water, on the sand. At one point, she pulled off her costume and ran about naked; but no one was going to worry about a naked three-year-old, least of all the Greeks.

Some sort of a photography competition was in action a little way off. I asked a waiter, who said it was organised by the municipality. Young men were photographing near-nude young women. I watched that with some interest until dozing off.

Violet roused me with a complaint that she had a stone in her paddling shoes. 'And it hurts my poor ickle toeses.' So I knelt down in the sand. Managing to remove the shoe, I shook out a pebble about the size of a well-built flea. The child then rushed back to the infant waves on the water's edge.

What misery my well-meaning care of that child brought me! I handed her over to Rosie on the terrace that evening. She seemed only moderately grateful for my self-sacrifice, whisking the child off for a bath, saying she had a headache and would retire early to bed.

Next morning, a chance remark made by a waiter to Rosie in my hearing revealed that she'd had not a sister to visit her on the previous day, but a male visitor. I challenged her immediately. Oh, he was just an old friend, nothing more. I did not believe her for a moment.

She took my arm and suggested I bought her a drink.

'You deceived me, didn't you? You used me. Don't deny it.'

'What else could I do?' She looked helpless, waved a hand a little to show how weak she was. 'He needed to see me on business matters. I needed some time with him, that was all.'

'Business matters? You must take me for a fool. He was here when I delivered Violet back to you, wasn't he? I believe he stayed overnight with you on these business matters.'

'No, no, please… It was not what you think.' Her dimples came into play.

Really, what do you expect? I stood up. I said I would discover at the reception desk if there had been a man with her all night. If they did not know, then I would ask a maid, or a night porter. I was determined to get at the truth.

She shifted from helplessness to anger. 'Do what you like, you fool! Do you imagine you own me? You had your turn! Find out what you like. Why should I care?'

It was that phrase, 'you had your turn' which I found so damaging, then and for a long while after.

So I too changed tack. 'Why should I care who you chose to sleep with? You can sleep with the night porter for all I care. It's the deviousness that disgusts me. If you had said that you had a lover visiting you, I'd have kept out of your way. I'd have understood. Why not be honest?'

She made a moue of contempt. 'Oh yes? If I had told you, you'd have started a row. You know you would. Because you were in love with me, or so you claimed.' She lit a cigarette with a grand, if rather dated, gesture. 'We went to bed together. Isn't that enough? Why always this talk of love? Love puts a claim on you. Why not simply the pleasure of it?'

A theatrical pause, then, 'Not that I gained much pleasure from you. You made so much noise about it. I was almost deafened. Does the entire hotel have to know when you're having a bloody orgasm? I hate all that.'

Like many a man in similar circumstances, I saw I was defeated.

'Rosie, you're an ungrateful bitch. I took care of your child, you hardly thanked me. You got us both out of the way all day. It was a mean trick. Don't you feel at all ashamed of deceiving me?'

She raised her eyebrows and blew smoke from her pretty lying lips. 'You told me you were glad to have Violet's company. If you weren't glad, then you were deceiving me! It was a convenient arrangement, that was all. Now let's stop discussing it, shall we?'

Of course, I was far too angry to stop discussing it.

Yet to go on would plunge me deeper into defeat. I hated her at that moment. I got up from my chair and headed for the outer door.

That was when she shrieked, to complete my humiliation, 'Besides, you shat over me, you bastard!'

I fled without a word. My cheeks burned as never before. Everyone in the foyer must have heard that final taunt. I walked along the front, that crowded front, full of people, baggage, buses, coaches, taxis, and Flying Dolphins. I could have flung myself into the sea – filthy though it was.

I sat myself down outside a small taverna, trying to recover my equilibrium. A waiter appeared at my elbow. I ordered an ouzo and a coffee. While I was sipping my drink, I watched without interest a man coming slowly through the crowd selling newspapers. He finally arrived at my table.

'English, mister?' he asked. No doubt I looked so uncomfortable that he knew of which nation I formed part: the poor beleaguered race inhabiting the island anchored on the north-west of Europe.

He offered me the English-speaking newspaper, *Athens News*. I bought a copy rather than endure the possibility of a hassle. I set it by my elbow. As I tipped the last of my ouzo down my throat and turned to call for another, I caught sight of a headline about the popularity of Aegina beaches. Beneath a photo was a line explaining that there had been a photographic competition on Marathonas beach yesterday. 'A father enjoys himself with his daughter on the beach'.

The picture was of me, kneeling by the naked Violet, fiddling with her shoe.

My first thought was: thank God I'm *not* her father. Then I could not help grinning. I didn't realise how close my face was to her little wee-wee. Lucky me that she had not taken it into her head to pee at that moment, as small kids are prone to do. I hadn't realised my danger.

Nor did I realise a greater danger.

I returned to England in time for the publication of my latest novel, *New Investments*, to encounter the worst trouble of my career. But you will remember the case. It is no fun for me to rake up the details again now. So we'll return to the Langstreets. They also had their troubles. Well, it wouldn't be a novel if they didn't.

Rather to Kathi's surprise, Paleohora seemed perfectly normal. Tourists were strolling about, shops were open, people sat outside tavernas and bars, relaxedly chatting. The sun shone down benignly on a slice of typical Mediterranean life.

Grim-faced, Langstreet enquired in a bar where the police station was. The barman looked blank. Police station? The nearest police station was in the mountains, in Kyriotisa. But there was an office here.

'My son was kidnapped here in Paleohora.'

The barman was sympathetic. There certainly was a local policeman; Takis by name. He lived in one of the side streets. Good-naturedly, the barman offered to take Langstreet to him. Calling to his waitress, who was sitting having a smoke on the verandah outside the bar, to take charge, he set out with Langstreet.

Kathi, meanwhile, had gone to speak to Vibe in her hotel, to hear her account of Cliff's capture. Vibe was dry-eyed and practical, and had already written a longhand account of what had happened. A van had been driving slowly along the front where Cliff and Vibe were lingering. They had paddled in the sea and were then on the road side of the promenade wall, kissing and discussing their next move – on the sand or back in Vibe's bed? The van stopped close to them and a man leaned out the window, asking Cliff for a light.

Cliff went over to him. As he was taking a folder of matches from his pocket, two men rushed around the front of the van and seized him. He struggled and yelled. They bashed his head against the cab and knocked him unconscious. Vibe attacked them, striking out with her shoe, which she had been carrying. Two more men jumped from the back of the van. They knocked her over. She was certain there were four men involved, one no more than adolescent, with a yellow kerchief tied round his head.

One of the men had kicked Vibe. She showed Kathi the bruise, high on her left thigh. Cliff had been bundled into the back of the van, which was then driven off at speed, towards the way out of town.

Had Vibe seen the number plate?

No. It had happened so fast. She had thought rather too late of taking the registration number, when the vehicle was already speeding away. It was dark. There were few street lights. She had the impression there was no rear number plate.

Kathi liked Vibe, with her intelligent and clear account. She took charge of the statement, bought her a drink and sympathised. She gave Vibe the phone number of their hotel. They kissed each other on parting.

Langstreet's barman, meanwhile, was knocking at a modest door, above which a sign said POLIS. It was situated in a side street close by the harbour. The door opened. A fat woman with a pleasant wrinkled face began to talk immediately. Quite a long conversation ensued. Langstreet stood by, concealing his impatience.

The chat concluded. The woman smiled at Langstreet, the door closed.

The barman said, 'She is mother of Takis. He live and work here below her room with his typewriter. Her daughter not too well with rather a back problem and two little childs. Takis, he is on his rounds. He can be at the bakery where his brother work. So we go there.'

They found Takis at the baker's, sitting at a little table, drinking

70

coffee and talking to his brother, who sat opposite to him, and his brother's wife, who stood silent by her husband's chair.

Since Takis spoke no more than a few words of English, another long conversation in Greek ensued, with the brother and his wife joining in occasionally. The woman left the group, to disappear into the rear quarters of the shop. She emerged a minute later with a coffee for Langstreet.

Accepting the cup, he said, 'Look, Mr Takis, this is urgent. My son has been kidnapped by a gang of thugs. Are you going to do something?'

The answer came through the barman. 'We do not have such crime in Paleohora. Therefore the men come from somewhere else. Probably foreigners. You must go to Kyriotisa. There they have a big station of police, with computers. There you can find help.'

More argument followed by all concerned. Langstreet set down the cup to make a small gesture of protest. He wanted Takis to check the harbour road for tyre prints. He was told that there was only one sort of tyre available locally.

The barman said, politely, that he must return to his bar for the midday trade.

Langstreet went back to his hotel. He was starting to throw some items of clothing and toiletry into an overnight bag, when Kathi entered the room.

'Archie, you walked right past me. I called to you. You ignored me. I'm as worried as you are, but be human, will you? What did the police say?'

'They said virtually nothing. Perhaps they know who my father was. Perhaps they also are against me. In Kyriotisa there's a real police station. I am going there. I'm packing in case I have to stay overnight. And I am sorry if I passed you by. There is much on my mind.'

'Stop packing for a moment, will you?' She went over and snapped the bag closed. She attempted to smile into his solemn face. 'Archie, I have Vibe's statement. She is a good, straightforward young woman. Also, I phoned the British Embassy in Athens. They are taking the matter seriously, thank God. They are going to send over an investigator who speaks Greek. He *is* Greek. He will help us. *And*, we may have received a message from the kidnappers.'

She produced a soiled brown envelope. She had retrieved it from their pigeonhole at the reception desk. The porter did not know who had put it there.

'Thank you, Kathi. How very sensible you are!' He moved forward and kissed her as he took the envelope. They stood together with their arms around each other. 'I can't help being anxious…'

He tore open the envelope with a thumbnail. Withdrawing a piece of lined paper, he read out its simple typed message:

We demand one million Deutschmarks for return of your son.

The note bore no signature. They stared at it gloomily without speaking. Then Langstreet tucked it slowly back into the envelope and put it in his pocket.

'What should we do?'

'We must phone this investigator to meet us in Kyriotisa. The message may provide a clue. Perhaps the make of typewriter can be identified from the printing. This is all so terrible.'

'Don't think of paying up, Archie. I spoke to Vibe. She said that during the scuffle, when the thugs were trying to get Cliff into the car, they called him a Kraut. It's in her statement.'

'So it is political! I feared as much. God, I was mad to bring us to this island. I must get to Kyriotisa at once.'

'If you imagine you're going without me you're much mistaken!'

'Yes, come too. I wasn't thinking… There's no danger.'

She gave a joyless laugh. 'So we thought…'

The outskirts of Kyriotisa lay dead and grey in the afternoon sun, as the re-hired Fiat Punto entered the town. There was some action at the service station, otherwise it seemed like a place embalmed. Nearer the centre of the straggling town, lorries and a few private cars were about. People wandered slowly in the street or the road.

Archie and Kathi recognised the advertisements for Coca Cola and Nentelstam Milk – 'Best for Babies', it said. By the side of the police station was a hoarding showing a yobbish young man with a cigarette in between his lips, and the legend, 'Get a Character – Get a Carter!' in English. They stopped the car and went in to see the police.

A man in jeans sitting at a computer – the very computer Takis had mentioned – put down a cigarette, presumably a Carter, and came over to them.

'You are from Paleohora? Takis phoned to me concerning your problem. Good evening. Your son has been taken, that's right? My name is Manolis Tsouderakis. I'm in charge here. Come and sit down to talk to me.'

It sounded like a promising start.

Manolis Tsouderakis was a clean-shaven man of about forty, and of medium height; his features were regular and sharp. Although his gaze was searching, he appeared to be well-disposed towards his visitors.

They sat down at a trestle table on which stood the computer and some stacks of paper. A uniformed man entered the office from the rear, and was sent off to get some coffee and wine.

Tsouderakis then made a performance of selecting paper and pen in preparation for taking a statement. Kathi presented him with Vibe's handwritten account. He read it through carefully, looking up to ask, 'Is this truthful? This woman was not an accomplice in the crime?'

'Certainly not.'

'She says that four crooks were involved in the abduction, eh? Mm. I had better interview her.'

'Do you know who these four men might be? Vibe says one was young and wore a yellow kerchief.'

'It's a gang, let's say. We are peaceful here. There are only a few such gangs…'

Langstreet handed over the ransom note in its brown envelope.

Tsouderakis appeared to weigh it in his hand before extracting the demand. He studied it for some while, saying nothing. The coffee came on a tray with a jug of wine, and was set on the table at his elbow.

When the Langstreets had reported on the little they knew between them about Cliff's abduction, the police chief got them to sign the statement.

He cleared his throat, nodded his head several times, and addressed them:

'I shall do all I can to help you in this crime. I am an educated man, you understand? I have degrees. Also, I have travelled beyond the confines of Crete and of Greece. It's a vital part of a man's education. I realise that some people in Kyriotisa are rather backward in their thinking.'

'Yes, yes,' said Langstreet, with impatience.

'Once I came to Poland and Germany. A friend from my family works in Mannheim. Mannheim's a good town, with decent people there.

'This I say to convince you that I have no feelings against Germans. They are a different generation now. However, the people of Kyriotisa are not greatly enlightened, let's say. They suffered harshly from German atrocities in the war.'

Tsouderakis began to enumerate some of these atrocities. It was a tale the Langstreets had heard on their separate visits to the town. Langstreet held up his hand. 'Excuse me, sir, but we know of these wartime misfortunes of half a century ago. We also understand that the German authorities made handsome restitution to Kyriotisa after the Nazis had been defeated. No point is served by bringing up these sad stories once more.'

Once more, Tsouderakis nodded his head as if in disagreement. Speaking slowly, he said, 'Excuse me, sir, but a point is served...' He paused before speaking again in a more formal voice, looking directly at Langstreet. 'For the purposes of this enquiry, I have to ask you directly if you are not the son of – and your son Clifford is not the grandson of – *Hauptsturmführer* Klaus Langenstrasse of the Waffen SS?'

A signal passed between Langstreet and his wife.

'Mr Tsouderakis, I feel this is a dangerous town in which to delve into the past…'

Manolis Tsouderakis suddenly became a more official person. Speaking with authority, he said, 'Dangerous or not, as you consider it, I have reason to believe that your father was a *Hauptsturmführer*, or captain, let's say, in the SS, and active in this very vicinity. If I am to help you, you had better tell the truth to me.'

Staring hard at the man, Langstreet said, 'This is an unfortunate question. I came to England as a boy of nine. I am English. I have an English name. England is my country. Also, I am a religious man. I reject my father and his ideology. I have nothing to do with Nazism – '

'But Klaus Langenstrasse was nevertheless your father?'

'Yes. He was.'

The hour was growing late. Dusk gathered in the banal room, as if the dusty history of Hitler's Third Reich was reassembling itself. As if whatever had been in the mind of young Klaus Langenstrasse had an essence that could still be felt; as if something in the baffling and quasi-messianic mind of Adolf Hitler had been experienced almost tangibly by his deceived subjects. Like his leader, Captain Klaus Langenstrasse held an absolute conviction regarding his goals.

The sorrowful end of this Cretan day was an acknowledgement that the melancholy circumstances of historic process were constantly uncoiling in this room.

Tsouderakis clicked on a desk lamp.

'There we have the reason for the abduction for your son. It may be this criminal gang expects to receive the ransom money demanded. However, I think it more likely that they understood very well that this capture would draw you back to Kyriotisa.'

Kathi's face was pale. She asked, 'Why should they want Archie back here?'

He clasped his hands together on the table and, staring at them, said, 'Maybe – this is just a theory – maybe they visited Paleohora to shoot you. They discovered you were not there. So they stole your son instead. Maybe they will shoot him up in the hills, let's say. They knew you had to come here to make your enquiries.

'Here, they can shoot you as you walk on the pavement. As your father used to do in the bad days.'

Langstreet looked extremely grim. He clutched the edge of the table. But his voice was steady when he spoke.

'Oh, this is villainous! Whatever my father's crimes were, they are not mine. I've done nothing. Cliff's done nothing. What could possibly be gained by shooting me?'

At this, Tsouderakis began a long explanation concerning the poverty existing in the town and region. Unemployment levels were high. The olive oil industry was run down. It operated on primitive machinery, and the oil had to be sold in barrels to Italy because of the lack of a bottling plant. People with nothing to do tended to turn to crime, in particular to theft and burglary. They were depressed. In some cases, they turned to violence. The events of the World War, though distant, could be used as an excuse for crime. Many men who had lost one parent or other during the German invasion still felt bitter; they had little else with which to fill their minds. It was a story that could be found elsewhere in the world. Perhaps the situation was aggravated here by the comparative isolation of Kyriotisa. The land was not very fertile. Another factor was that there was a tradition of resistance to foreigners; Kyriotisa had been a centre of resistance against the Ottoman power, long before the Nazi invaders. Business invest-ment – even a tourist industry, if such a thing were possible – would greatly benefit everyone, and lead immediately to a reduction in misery and lawlessness.

To this long analysis, the Langstreets listened with resignation.

At the end of it, Langstreet repeated his question, asking what could be gained by his being shot.

'The wrong-doers would say that they avenged an ancient wrong. The ancient philosophy of an eye for an eye… They would be seen by others as powerful people, to be feared… Do not worry, Mr Langstreet, I will see to it you are not shot, or your wife. My wife runs a little domatia or pension, let's say, nearby. You must stay there for the night.'

'Wouldn't it be safer to drive back to Paleohora?' Kathi asked.

'If these criminals know you are here, as is likely the case, then they can attack your car just outside the town. Stay here and be safe.'

The assistant was then summoned. He took the fingerprints of the visitors in a businesslike manner. Tsouderakis, in a friendly fashion, said he would take them by the back way to his mother's house. The luggage in their car would be collected for them. But first, he would show them how Langstreet had been identified as the son of his father.

He led them into one of the rear rooms. Here were stored photographs of the Cretan patriotic struggle against Fascism. Kathi refused to look at the gory collection. Captured on Kodak Brownie cameras in black-and-white were pictures of heads severed from bodies, of naked men and women hanging from ropes, of people with terrible mutilations, and of German troops. And of *Hauptsturmführer* Klaus Langenstrasse in military uniform, standing in the middle of a road, with a service revolver pointed against a boy's head.

Langstreet gave a convulsive sob. The profile of his father was so similar to his own. The steep brow, the craggy nose, the thin lips and the square jaw: these were his as they were his father's. Staring at the photograph, he could feel only sorrow that his father had been led so far away from God that he could commit such crimes. His father would suffer in hell for what he had done.

'That's enough,' he said.

77

Kathi clutched his hand as Manolis Tsouderakis led them through the back door into a dark alleyway.

After they had eaten with the wizened Mrs Tsouderakis and their luggage had been delivered, the Langstreets retired to a small back room allocated to them. It was sparsely furnished but clean. Archie went down on his knees, locked his hands together, and prayed silently by the side of the bed. Kathi sighed, standing there staring at her husband's bowed head.

When he rose, she asked, 'Why should God listen to you? Did he listen to the small boy in the photograph, the boy your father was about to shoot? ... No, sorry, I'm sorry I asked that. Never question faith!'

'Faith is greater than reason, Kathi,' he said gently.

'Maybe that's why I'm on reason's side.'

At two in the morning, they were lying together in the bed, awake. He spoke. 'A tourist industry! Is that really a cure for the sins of mankind?' His tone implied that the question, being rhetorical, required no answer.

Nor did it receive any.

When I was first learning my trade as a writer, I read Henry Fielding's novel, *Joseph Andrews*. What I most enjoyed was the way in which Fielding would alternate chapters of narrative with chapters of discussion about what was happening in his book. He adopted a relaxed and man-of-the-world style, rather as if a friend of your father's was talking with you over a glass of claret.

Well, such were my impressions of the book. However, when I took up my copy again after many years (so many that the book contains, inside its front cover, a little old-fashioned booksellers' tab, announcing that it came from Sanders & Co, Booksellers, 104 High St Oxford) I found this division of chapters was not as regular as I had remembered them to be. It is always disconcerting to find that past reality was not that real – however often the discovery occurs. What do you expect? I asked myself.

This habit of Fielding's of tackling the reader head on would now be categorised as post-modernism, or is it deconstruction, or something? Whatever label you may put on it, I might perhaps remark here – emboldened by Fielding's admittedly fading example – on the different ways in which people adapt to disasters in early life. Just take the current cases; the more villainous citizens of Kyriotisa, and Archie Langstreet.

The post-war government in the new Germany was enlightened. It did its best to make amends for Nazi atrocities and showed, I believe, genuine penitence regarding the crimes of the Third Reich. In the case of Kyriotisa, this penitence was demonstrated by the practical step of rebuilding much of the town.

However, in the light of our present knowledge, we might judge that a more effective course would have been to send in teams of psychiatrists, with which Germany was at one time well-stocked, to deal with the wide incidence of post-traumatic stress. Counselling, mothering, what-you-will, might have alleviated the worst of the sorrows from which the inhabitants suffered. This benevolence might not have been entirely successful – it could never restore a leg, or a wife or daughter – but it might have been seen as less triumphalist than a granite war memorial with raised lettering. Then again, what would I know?

The compulsion to pour out their woes to strangers, half a century after the event, shows how the citizens of this unfortunate town still suffered from their nightmare.

By contrast, Archie Langstreet had had to suppress his woes, although they, by and large, stemmed from the same horrific incidents. He had received no counselling either. When Archie arrived in England, a small, displaced lad, in the last years of the forties, post-traumatic stress disorder was unheard of, otherwise half of the population of Britain would have been queuing for counselling. So Archie had grown into an upright man, religious, driven to achieve justice where he saw injustice, and only an occasional tic to show for the sublimation.

> Some fall apart where others seem to mend;
> We bow the head and do not comprehend.

As to my own troubles, I hardly comprehended where they sprang from. I had so often, to use the popular phrase, 'got away with murder', and now I was being publicly blamed for a vile crime I had not committed.

Bloody publicity! Everywhere you look there's talk about sex. There's no refuge, even when your – er, read *my* libido is failing. No doubt this is all a side effect (you might say a backside effect) of the invention of the Pill in the sixties, when suddenly all those juicy little quims became more easily available, and panties fell like ripe apples off trees.

Boris came to see me a week after my novel, *New Investments*, was published. On his face was a mean sort of sheepish-triumphant grin. He handed me a tabloid newspaper. The front page of the *Comet* bore the headline, PAEDOPHILE WRITER'S PUBLIC CRIME. Below it was the study of me on the Aegina beach, with my innocent face almost between innocent Violet Herbage Potts' little stumps of legs.

I rang Sidney Quarrell, my lawyer. I fixed an appointment with him.

His offices were bright and almost up-to-date. I awaited Quarrell's pleasure in a spacious outer office occupied by a secretary and a receptionist, who sat at white melanite desks, murmuring occasionally into phones. On the walls of mushroom tone – the decor was of that vintage – were framed and innocuous abstracts, printed in not more than two colours. Below the window, which looked out on the backs of older buildings, was a plastic trough containing real flowers.

Being restless, I approached the flowers.

'Don't touch the geraniums!' cried receptionist and secretary as one.

Too late. I had touched. A shock rushed up my hand and arm to my shoulder and then to my heart. I let out a grunt of surprise.

'It's static electricity,' said the receptionist, getting up smartly to see that I was all right – lawyers hate to have people dying on their premises. 'Sorry. Thelma and I forgot to water the carpet this morning.'

'Sick building syndrome?'

' 'Fraid so. Let me get you a glass of water, sir.'

'Better pour it on the carpet, perhaps?'

Allowed in to see Sidney, I spent a good part of the morning in his sanctum, talking, throwing in a bit of gesticulation here and there, to show him I was human even if he wasn't. Old Quarrell, with his withered lawyer's face, was discouraging. He advised against writing a letter of complaint to the newspaper, or trying to clear my name through the medium of the Society of Authors. Nor could I afford to sue the *Comet* for libel. The trial would only bring me more adverse publicity.

Quarrell laid a gentle hand on a copy of *New Investments*, which he had by him on his desk. I knew the cost of it would appear on my next bill.

'There are passages in this novel of yours,' he said, 'which an opposing lawyer would seize upon in order to launch a counter-attack on your morals. I refer to certain paragraphs in the early chapters, where a small boy has romps with his Polynesian nurse. Also, on page – ah, yes, ninety-one, you refer to Russian peasants sucking the penises of their sons. Would you not classify that as paedophile activity?'

'No, not at all. Our bloody modern world is paedophile mad. Look, Sidney, one of the characters, my garrulous guy Arnold, quotes this custom as something the Russian peasantry totally accepted, bizarre as it might seem. It was their primitive way of calming their sons. I suppose they found it worked. When twenty of you live together in some squalid hut on the steppes... What do you expect?

'The trouble is, you don't understand fiction. It's nothing I've done. Sucking the dirty little cock of a Russian peasant's son comes very far down my list of pleasures. I can assure you of that.'

'But could you assure the court?'

'I read about this and other obnoxious habits in a book by Orlando Figes called *A People's Tragedy*. Jolly good book. I stuck it into a discussion of the state of present-day Russia, didn't I? Just to look a bit knowledgeable.'

I tried to explain to him the way writers worked, relying much on serendipity. Even if an author had his theme and his conclusion firmly in mind, nevertheless, when a plum happened to come along – say in conversation or in reading – then into the novel it went, to flavour the pudding. It need not be about anything the writer actually knew or did. Indeed, the more novelty the plum had, the more likely it was to make an impression and be added as enrichment to the mix.

Quarrell listened to this without changing his expression, as though he had become a waxwork of himself. Then he spoke again.

'And what about the Polynesian nurse?'

I might as well have saved my breath.

'Well, I certainly had a Polynesian nurse as a kid... These "romps", as you put it, were all things she did to me. What do you expect? It was much like the case of Lord Byron, whose nurse "interfered with his person". I served up this last phrase in a creditable Scots accent.

Quarrell was far from being amused.

'Thus the paedophile is born. Or so your *Comet* lawyer would argue. Whatever the truth may be, regarding this photo with the small girl on a Turkish beach – '

'Greek.'

' – on a Greek beach, and I can see some force in your argument that it shows you in an innocent if unfortunate position, the *Comet*'s legal team will turn what you have written against you.'

In a feeble attempt at light-heartedness, I asked, 'But how did you like the novel, Sidney? A good read, *n'est ce pas*?'

He leant forward a little and smiled the way an eagle smiles. 'I am not here to deliver literary opinions. If you wish my advice, I would advise you to rent a cottage in Cornwall until it all blows over. And do not speak to reporters.'

It worries me to this day to imagine how the *Comet* got hold of that confounded picture. Did they subscribe to *Athens News*? Or did someone send them a copy of the paper?

Could it possibly have been Lady Rosemary de Vere, in a fit of vindictiveness? Just because I shat on her?!

Chapter Five

It was Thursday. Archie Langstreet had to be back in Geneva on the Saturday, since the first meeting of lawyers on both sides of the Nentelstam lawsuit was to take place on the Monday. Co-ordination was required before the meeting.

Mrs Tsouderakis gave him and Kathi a breakfast of boiled eggs and bread, followed by yoghurt. Manolis had already left for his office.

The wife was a plump woman with an apron, pristine white, tied about her middle. She smiled regularly upon her visitors, in a pleasant way. She spoke to them in Greek, and poured milk from a stoneware jug.

She let them out of her back door into the alleyway. Morning sun slanted in at the far end of the lane, embracing worn stonework and blistered doors. An atmosphere of slightly unfocused peace was engendered, as in a painting by Chardin. Massed marigolds draped themselves over a wall. A young woman was sweeping her doorstep, watched by a cat lying some feet away in a patch of sun.

'Perhaps when you've slept in a place you begin to like it,' Kathi said.

'Or failed to sleep?' Langstreet spoke with a wry smile, but his face was pale and drawn.

They banged on the metal rear door of the police station and were promptly admitted.

Manolis Tsouderakis was cheerful. 'I think already we get somewhere,' he said. He showed them the ransom note, on which he had underlined the three 'm's in the message. They fell slightly aslant on the paper. He snatched up a typewritten letter on his desk, offering it for comparison.

'This is a letter written by the local garage owner to a customer three years ago. You see how the 'm's are slanting in the same way as on the ransom note. It is one and the same typewriter. It was stolen from the garage.'

'This helps us find Cliff?'

'Exactly. There was working at the garage a young man, young but heavy. He disappeared on the day the typewriter disappeared. We know his name. Stathis Vlachos, a thief. He was not from here at birth. We know he lives in the mountains. He comes down to Kyriotisa sometimes to rob.'

'You don't arrest him?'

'Is a little difficult. But now we go and seek him and find your son and then we arrest him. First we will wait for some reinforcements.'

They waited. Tsouderakis worked on other matters, and spoke soothingly to a middle-aged woman who came in to complain about the noise of a bar next to her rooms. Kathi wished to go out and take a walk, but was advised against it.

After an hour's wait, a smart Land Cruiser drew up outside. Into the office a police captain marched with ponderous step. Following him came two tough-looking men in camouflage uniforms. The captain had a revolver in a holster at his hip. The men carried carbines. The captain did his best to look overbearing; he was certainly tall and inclined to fat. He took a turn about the office, glaring here and there, nodding to himself as if detecting invisible fingerprints. His cheeks wobbled when he spoke. Kathi immediately had a name for him: the Iron Jelloid.

The Iron Jelloid shook hands with Langstreet, while completely ignoring his wife. He then stood, legs apart, arms folded across his chest, blank seriousness written across his face, as if thinking to himself, *These foreigners will see that I am a man to contend with.*

'These are our reinforcements from Hania,' Tsouderakis announced. 'We are obliged to them for their prompt arrival. We are in the Hania province. I will go with these two men to capture Vlachos in the hills. Mr Langstreet, you can come with me. Mrs Langstreet, you stay here. You will be safe under the eye of the Hania Captain Maderakis, who will guard you and the office while I am absent.'

When Kathi began to protest, Langstreet said he did not want her to be exposed to danger, and requested her to remain behind. She stayed reluctantly, eyeing the Iron Jelloid. He settled himself in an old wicker chair, which creaked like a rotten branch under his weight. He grunted and rested his booted feet on the edge of Tsouderakis' desk. Silence enveloped him. He removed a Filofax from a breast-pocket and began to leaf through it slowly.

After the others had slammed out of the office, Kathi spoke in order to break the ice.

'This is what happens in all the cowboy films. The men gallop off to the shoot-out, while the little woman stays back at the ranch, brewing coffee. I didn't realise till now how true to life it all was.'

The Iron Jelloid said nothing. He glanced up. Then he continued to study his Filofax. Finally, he tucked it away with impressive sloth.

From an inner pocket, he produced a mobile phone and talked into it at length, all the while staring at Kathi. The talk concluded; he tucked the phone away again.

With clumsy fingers, he extracted a cigarette from a packet of Carters, lighting it in a soulful manner with a green plastic lighter. Kathi sat sideways on a chair, resting her chin in her hand. She gazed at a shelf full of old files.

Maderakis said, 'You know nothing of my former history. I am an enigma before you. You can admit that.'

Not wishing to know, Kathi kept quiet.

'I am a gourmet and an intellectual. It is not everyone who is touched by genius. This means something. I am not simply a policeman, as you may feel disposed to imagine.' He forced a laugh-like noise. 'I have a character, you know.'

The statement could have been designed to make Kathi feel comfortable in his presence. Or uncomfortable. She remained mute.

'It is not always seldom that idleness meets wickedness, in my career. The unexpected goes on – though not in my thoughts. Perhaps you are disappointed that your holiday has taken this adverse turn.'

She remained silent no longer. 'Of course I'm disappointed. More than that, I am furious and worried out of my mind. Not only is Cliff in danger, but now your local policeman has taken my husband out with his men into the mountains, so that he's in danger too. What do you expect me to be but anxious?'

The massive cheeks wobbled slightly. 'Reading the notes my subordinate faxed me overnight, with demanded efficiency, I see that the facts of the case were such. You left your injured husband to be with a monk. Again, another factor, Clifford Langstreet is not your son. So I question myself as if a malefactor: why are you so overwrought?'

'Overwrought? Who said I was overwrought? For your information, I love Cliff as if he were my son. Do you find that surprising?'

He puffed out a Carter's smoke signal and watched it rise with grave suspicion.

'You raise the subject of love, but there I regret we must disagree. People do not naturally love. We are things apart, as I could say I am a thing apart. Love is an affectation of civilisation. We can learn it like speech. I may say I love my job, but that is only a figure of speech. In fact, I merely do my duty forever. I might claim I loved you. In fact, I merely lust after you. I might say – '

She stood up. 'Oh, I've had enough of this. Shut up, will you? Is this why you stayed behind, simply to rile me? Go outside and have a smoke, will you?'

He brought his feet to the floor with a crash and raised himself massively from his chair. 'Naturally, I will do what you wish. It's not harmful to be polite. You, after all, are a foreign lady, and so naturally distressed. I have been to your country. I saw it very well, all the buildings, small and big. The Tower. I will smoke something outside. My endeavour was merely to calm you with some conversation, to strike up a possible friendship. My regrets that this is not possible, and probably never will be in this world.'

As he spoke, he was making heavily for the door. As soon as Maderakis was gone, Kathi regretted she had spoken in such a tactless manner. After all, he was a man with some power in a land she perceived as increasingly hostile; she should not have risked offending him.

She went to the door. The Hania captain stood outside in a heroic pose, lifting his cigarette above his head after each inhalation.

She said that she regretted speaking sharply. It was because she was allergic to cigarette smoke.

'And much else, probably, madam,' Maderakis said. 'If you saw the film called *Easy Rider*, all is explained there. The fear of smoke brings cancer, no doubt. But what is courage, after all, in this age?'

'Quite,' she agreed.

The Iron Jelloid looked down on Kathi, eyes swivelled over his large cheeks, with some contempt.

'You tell me to be quiet. You cannot silence my thoughts. In my thoughts I solve the crimes of the present. I destroy the bad. Also all those abominable crimes as yet not committed, murder, rape, incest – they are crushed in my thoughts and squeezed dry of essence. I go through them one by one, as with your son. Your nearly son.'

His phone buzzed, muffled by his coat. 'Here must end our conversation. It's important.'

'Oh, thank you,' she said, backing away. She retired to the office and smoked a cigarette, holding her arms against her body.

The sun went through its daily routine of looking over the mountains at Kyriotisa and its large war memorial. By three in the afternoon, it was shining in the two narrow windows of the police station.

It was at about that time that the Land Cruiser returned. Manolis Tsouderakis entered his station, looking pleased. Behind came the two policemen in camouflage outfits, escorting a ragged and hand-cuffed youth – a grim-looking trio; while Langstreet entered last, appearing depressed.

'We have captured this vagabond, Stathis Vlachos, and he will be imprisoned after trial.'

This was said rather grandly to Captain Maderakis. He immediately took out his mobile phone and commenced a loud conversation. Kathi asked Tsouderakis, 'And Cliff?'

Langstreet answered, 'No sign of the kidnappers. A waste of time. No sign even of the typewriter.'

'So why have you arrested this man?' Kathi asked Tsouderakis, glancing at the handcuffed Vlachos.

'Because he stole the typewriter in the first place!'

Maderakis came forward, taking command. 'Now I interrogate him to extract the truth. Stathis Vlachos, you impede the course of law. Where is now the missing typewriter you have hidden away?'

Vlachos was a broken-mouthed individual. He wore rough clothes and a rougher haircut. His manner was crestfallen. Nevertheless, he spoke up boldly. 'I am a shepherd now. I have nothing to do with crime. Only with sheep and goats.'

'Your ovine concerns are outside my compass. I have no faith in them, because they are discardable. You do more good for humanity to work in a garage and mend cars. Now, fellow, answer my question about the missing typewriter. Did you burn it? Did you bury it?'

'The kidnappers came to my house, four of them,' the youth replied. 'They threatened to beat me up. They stole my best billy-goat and my typewriter.'

'What of your old mother?'

'I have no old mother.'

The Iron Jelloid looked thoughtful, and stroked his chin. 'Not of itself any proof of guilt, maybe... But you could be lying.'

Tsouderakis said brightly, 'So tomorrow we go back into the hills. The typewriter will help us to identify the kidnappers.'

'I imagine that the presence of my son will help too,' Langstreet said.

Like Sherlock Holmes, I am a master of disguise. I adopted a false moustache.

I was looking at Virginia Woolf's essays while wondering what was going to happen next to the Langstreets. Nowadays, some of Woolf's essays seem a little precious, a little hoity-toity. They were written three-quarters of a century ago. She was a good critic, her best critical pieces being contained in the two books of *The Common Reader*.

One of her pieces is entitled, 'How Should One Read a Book?' I turned to it eagerly, because I had hopes that Woolf would offer some advice about reading a book while wearing a false moustache. The trick is not as easy as you might think. The damned thing tickles.

It turns out that such practical matters are beneath Woolf's notice. She says, '...if you open your mind as widely as possible, these signs of almost imperceptible fineness, from the twist and turn of the first sentences, will bring you into the presence of a human being unlike any other.'

While admiring what Woolf says, I cannot help wondering if my sentences twist and turn sufficiently. And, more pertinently, if I am a human being unlike any other. Does the fact that I write make me a being apart?

While I have my doubts about that, I certainly felt like a being apart when, taking Sidney Quarrell's advice, I rented out my London flat and went to stay at a small hotel in Broadway, in the Cotswolds, for a month. Here it was that I adopted the false moustache.

I soon became extremely bored. Anyone with whom I endeavoured to have a conversation seemed to be living back in the Dark Ages of the 1930s. Although I regard myself as rather a common sort of fellow, I was convinced that Virginia Woolf would have been no happier with the company than I. Most of the women passing through the foyer of the hotel were heavily powdered, wore jodhpurs, and had rather sizeable bottoms. Their men folk wore Norfolk jackets and strutted about with their hands in their jacket pockets. Both sexes talked in loud, honking voices. One assumed they were aping a bygone aristocracy.

This factor may or may not be connected with the way in which the side tables in the lounge were stocked with copies of *The Field*, *Horse and Hounds*, and *Hunting & Other Cruel Sports*.

Not only was I unable to endure this arrogance; I grew tired of watching the entrance for anyone having an air of looking for convicted criminals. Much of my time was spent in my room, that cosy room with its chintz curtains decorated with horseshoes, or engaged in that most tedious of occupations, *walking*. There is something about fresh air which saps the creative processes. Fresh air, after all, is where all this hunting and other cruel sports are staged.

It is not environmentally friendly – or not in my environment.

I could find nothing worth reading in the little Broadway book-shop, since I did not intend to breed foxhounds, cook for twelve, or mingle with the Royal Family. In these uncongenial Cotswold surroundings, it was impossible to continue with my Cretan book although, when in London, I had been in full spate, greatly looking forward to revealing the moral of the whole story.

Suffering from the deserts of writer's block, I struck up a

conversation with the man who ran a small newsagent's shop. Small it was; claustrophobia ruled. One wall was covered with garish magazines. Most of them specialised in one subject only – health, diet, motorcycles, yachting, sex, fashion, computers, hunting, home decor, gardens. Presumably they were consumed by my enemies, the people who did not or could not read real books.

There were, I noted, no family magazines, such as *The Passing Show*, which I had enjoyed as a boy. These specialised journals were produced for a fragmented society.

The owner, tucked behind his counter in his patterned cardigan, looked morose. I thought him prematurely aged, until I found he was in his late seventies.

'I should have retired long ago,' he said, shaking his grey head. 'But my wife's disabled and we've got her mum to look after. It's rheumatism and lupus, mainly. I have to keep going here as long as I can.'

'Is that very difficult? You seem cosy enough in here.'

'I have to get up at four-thirty every morning, to get the rounds going. It's *Times* and *Telegraph* they read, mainly, round here. It takes it out of you, day in, day out. Sometimes Trixie's brother Gary will take over for a week in the summer – gives me a break. I take her to Weston-super-Mare. We're friendly with a woman as keeps a boarding house there. She's packing it in next year. Gets a lot of drunks in nowadays, she says. We're quiet. Don't drink. Can't afford it.'

I nodded towards his racks of magazines.

'At least you have plenty to read when business is slack. I see you've got a lot of porn magazines on your top shelf.'

'Aye, *Asian Babes* and all that filth. I thought you'd get round to that, sooner or later. I can recognise your type soon as I see them coming through that door. You can tell by the moustache. No offence, of course. But they're disgusting trash – them young-sters showing off their sexual quarters and their arseholes. They should be kept private, the way my generation used to do. Young girls of sixteen… Not a stitch on.'

'Does it shock you?'

'It shocks Trixie, I'll tell you that. *Tasty* is the worst, she says. Two young things in the swaer-nerf position, I don't know.'

'Is there much demand for them?'

'Not from locals there isn't. Tourists buy them. This used to be a respectable town, did Broadway.'

'I see. Well, I'll just take this copy of *Asian Babes*, thanks.'

He was correct. The young ladies certainly did exhibit the things he mentioned to the public at large.

While I was lingering in Broadway, my literary agent sent me a few pounds in royalties from Wilberforce Large, my publishers, together with a few pence from Malpractice and Sims, one of my earlier publishers. There was also a note reminding me that my novel was overdue. I could not determine if Welling-Jones, my agent, was referring to the novel I was writing, the one I was intending to write, or one I had never written. Sometimes a feeling of hopelessness overcomes you.

I dropped him a postcard with a view of Broadway, asking if he thought I was mad.

Back came a note saying he had always thought it. That made me laugh.

But supposing the universe had been especially designed to make people mad. Unlikely though it seems, the human species has developed from something that mucked about in trees and fecundated its partners in trees. Although we have abandoned this latter rather tricky habit, our species has developed societies which impose maximum strain on individuals, wearing them out, disillusioning them, as speedily as possible. Questions have become unavoidable on such fraught matters as how an ape-like person is supposed to enjoy a constant sex life, or maintain a decent standard of prose, or earn a penny to keep body and soul together.

My life of exile was livened up rather unpleasantly when Sidney Quarrell's office forwarded a letter with a film studio heading, signed by Sylvia Beltrau.

It took me a while to recall that Sylvia Beltrau was the screen name of my son Boris' little Lucia, with whom cunnilingus, as reported, had been so pleasurable.

She'd sent me an informal and spiteful little note, warning me to expect a solicitor's letter. The note began, 'Dear Paedophile', and accused me of having sex with her when she was underage. She claimed it had warped her life. She demanded recompense, and was preparing to smear my name and my face across the news journals and TV screens of the world. Not to mention the World Wide Web...

I was in what could be construed as a panic. I rang a pal of mine in London, Bernie 'Bodger' Smith, who wrote film biographies and knew erotic Hollywood details, such as how many lovers the exotic love goddess Hedy Lamarr had had in her lifetime (information I treasured). Despite this erudition, he seemed somewhat stumped by what I had actually been up to with young Sylvia.

'What's cunnilingus?'

'It's what a phonologist might call 'mastering the labials'.'

After a lengthy pause, he said, in a rather guttural way, 'I see. From the Latin, *cuntius*, a cunt, and *lingere*, to lick.'

I was impressed. Bernie had never been to university.

It turned out later that he knew this activity under the old name of 'gamming', from the French verb, *gamaruche*.

For a while, we discussed how you went about it. It occurred to me that Bernie was rather an amateur, more inclined to take head than give it.

'Is it PC to ask her first, do you reckon?'

'Yes,' I said. 'But did you ever meet a woman who said no?'

'What about if she's having a period?'

'Admittedly, that's rather an acquired taste.'

Old Bernie liked to pose as a man about town. 'You're paying for this call,' he said, 'so I'll tell you a joke. It's about how to impress your lover. If you're a man trying to impress a woman, you send her flowers, take her out shopping, buy her something expensive, write her a love letter or two – I suppose that means emails these days – more flowers, more compliments. Then you may get lucky. If you're a woman trying to impress a man, you just turn up naked with a crate of beer.'

His laughter rattled down the phone like gunfire. I had heard the joke before.

He provided me with one of the underlying reasons why Sylvia Beltrau had chosen this moment to strike. Her new motion picture drama, *Something to Behold*, was about to be launched. Doubtless her thought was that a little scandal would assist promotion of the movie. What do you expect?

'Did you really get your face in her fanny when she was sixteen?'

'Bernie, it was all an accident. I didn't know her age, had no idea. In any case, the organ in question was well-developed.' I found myself repeating the description, rather lingeringly. 'Well-developed... She insisted I went down on her. It wasn't a moment to be asking questions exactly. I never intended to do such a thing. It just looked so inviting...' (I set down these words of mine in good faith, believing, hoping, that the truth should be known about ourselves, however bad it is, so that we can still be accepted as a paid-up member of the human race: to admit all our folly and weakness, *yet become loved, or still be loved...*)

(Or if you can't love me, show some respect. Ignore the false moustache. I was once short-listed for the Booker.)

Perhaps my pal Bodger Smith, in his light-hearted response, showed he did accept all my folly and weakness. Perhaps they were his follies and weaknesses too, revealed when he spoke again.

'Lucky bugger! I bet you wish you could do it again, don't you?'

I licked my lips. 'I don't think that way. What am I to do?'

His laughter came down the phone line. 'You'd better make yourself scarce, old boy. Why not hide out in the Cotswolds?'

'Damn it, I am hiding out in the Cotswolds.'

There is no doubt that paedophiles are highly unpopular in our society. One can read something to their detriment in the papers every day. I do not espouse their cause, if they have one. But if any reader has the cheek to be disgusted, I will say that we read books, fiction in particular, not only to satisfy those yearnings we know about, but also to uncover those yearnings we have hitherto concealed from ourselves.

And another thing. My dead darling, Polly Pointer, a principled woman if ever I met one, was superintendent of a children's home. She loved me. She loved the children, and protected them. Yet she admitted to me, in one of our intimate moments, that, after she had been bathing a small boy, and was towelling him dry, his little willie perked up; it looked so inviting that she had it in her mouth before she could stop herself. She immediately pulled away and continued to dry the child. Yet the fleeting contact so disturbingly seized on a dark part of her imagination that she had to retire to her room and masturbate herself.

She never again bathed the children, but delegated the duties to underlings – supervised underlings.

Polly believed that the child in adults, even mature adults, was soothed by sucking. Sucking carried echoes of the placations of the maternal breast. Or, in some cases, of the breast's denial. As, for instance, those who were fobbed off with a bottle and formula milk, as a substitute for the breast.

In my hideout, I sat down and composed a letter to Sylvia Beltrau, requesting her not to proceed with prosecution.

'You may recall,' I wrote, 'that you were in a state of sexual excitement, and invited me to please you in the way you wished, that is to say, with my mouth to your genitals. I had no idea of your age, only that you behaved like a woman, and your womanly parts were well-developed. They were fresh, prettily shaped, prettily coloured – I recall them still – and I caught your scent. I believe you knew even at that early period of your life that few men could resist your invitation.

'Do you make our actions public because you despise them? I hope not. Cunnilingus seems to me a loving act, an act of trust, not to be despised. I felt you melt under my lips, so that we became liquid things. I was so lost that – will this surprise you? – my erection ceased to play a part in our communication; I sought no other gratification, did I?' (A bit of a lie, that.) 'I could, from my privileged position, survey your mons, your body, your distant breasts which you clutched, your lovely face. In the act, I felt… my emotions were turbulent, but what I felt was nearer an act of worship than of lust.

'I did not defile myself, I did not defile you. Please do not try to make capital out of our mutual pleasure.'

I let the letter lie about for a day. Then I tore it up.

She would never have worn it.

Well, I'd better get on with the Cretan teat story. That is one consolation about being a writer: you can always submerge yourself in a novel, and hope it has no connection with your real life.

Perhaps I will move things on a bit and cut the next episode short.

On the following morning, Nikolis Fraghiadakis arrived, smartly dressed in an impressive black car. This was the agent sent by the British Embassy in Athens, and a formidable little figure he cut. But little he certainly was, wearing high-heeled shoes to prove it. What he lacked in height, he made up in chest, and in a flamboyant manner.

He greeted Langstreet and Kathi 'in full cognisance…', 'sympathetically aware…', 'wishing to divulge his concern…', 'more than delighted to give his assistance…', and yes, he would accept a coffee – 'plus a raki if available' – while Langstreet, Manolis and Captain Maderakis (whose first name turned out to be Yiorgos) gave him all pertinent information on the case.

'The latest development,' Langstreet told him, 'has been a renewed ransom demand, sent to our hotel in Paleohora. It contains a photograph, so the hotel informs us, of Clifford, rather amateurishly taken, which seems to show him with a black eye. The note demands half of the money – that is, half a million Deutschmarks – by tomorrow evening.'

'We'll round them up today, have no fear,' said Nikolis Fraghiadakis, nodding at the Jelloid in collusion. 'It's terrible that innocent tourists should suffer in this way. It is as though war is still being waged. I fear that the hatred of Germany fills ignorant minds yet. Last week, I was holidaying in a small town with a lady friend of mine. We had a pleasant room in the main square. On the morning of our first day, I heard a noise in the square. So I look out, and what do I see?'

He spread wide his hands, lapsing into the present tense.

'I see the Wehrmacht enter into the square. They are in force. First tanks come – the good old Tiger, you know; I'm sure you remember, Mr Langstreet – following by lorries and field guns… How would you say it? Howiters? And then platoons of men, doing the goose step! And of course they have the flag with the swastika flying. I am horrified. Maybe they hid out in the White Mountains and never surrendered. So I call to my woman. She comes, takes one look, and begins to scream. The screams are very very loud. I try to stop her, for fear they might shoot from the square, you know? But she has lost her father to the Nazis when she was very young – executed before her eyes. So I have to stuff my vest in her mouth to shut her up – in her own inter-ests, you understand. The tanks come to a halt beneath our window. I, even I, am much afraid. But the landlady of the premises, she hears the cries of my woman and up she comes, to reassure us that it is only a film being made by Director Panayiotu, a film of history. So then we feel less bad. We are safe from danger. But my weekend is spoilt because my woman has become withdrawn and frankly, I feel to myself, a little silly about it. She cannot stand the Nazi uniform, even when it is just worn by an actor.'

During this monologue, Langstreet had risen from his chair and paced about the room, arms folded over his chest.

Kathi flared up. 'Why are you telling us this stupid story? What has it to do with the matter at hand? Surely you must see how insensitive it is! Are you trying to insult my husband?'

Fraghiadakis sat bolt upright, and expanded his chest. 'Of course no insult. The story must be of interest to your husband, since he is German by origin, is he not?'

'What has that got to do with it?'

'It has very much to do. Your step-son has been kidnapped because of it.'

'Oh my God, this is like being in a lunatic asylum!' exclaimed Kathi. Langstreet came and laid a gentle hand on her shoulder.

'Never mind the foolish story, my love,' he said. Directing his gaze at Fraghiadakis, he added, 'Now that your recitation is over, now you have got it off your chest, let us consider what the plan of action is. Yiorgos, you believe you know where these hostage-takers hide out?'

The Iron Jelloid captain was glad to speak:

'During the night, we questioned our captive, Vlachos, extensively. At about two-thirty this morning, he admitted that the villains are very probably hiding out in a small village called Frasas. Not an important village for vegetables or philosophy. The village has been deserted, since all inhabitants left for a bigger town, forced by poverty so rife here. Maybe they go to seek for vegetables, maybe philosophy, maybe even work. I suggest we leave here promptly, because we shall have an hour, or maybe two, of rough driving ahead of us, before we reach the place.'

'Do you know this place, Frasas?'

'I know it well. There is a mountain to the south, under which the village shelters. We can survey it from there, and then move in.'

'Good. Kathi, will you please stay here, to be safe?'

'I want to come with you, Archie. Would I be safe here, or would some madmen – plentiful in these parts, it seems – break in and capture me? Please don't leave me again. Please, Archie!'

He stroked her face and apologised for getting her into a mess. Of course she could come with them.

'We will not let you get shot, madam,' said Nikolis Fraghiadakis, condescendingly. 'It bears no part in our plans.'

Archie and his wife were in the back of the last vehicle in a line of three. Yiorgos Maderakis, the Iron Jelloid, sat in the front with the driver, wrapped, not only in his thoughts but a large, black, leather raincoat. Although the sun shone as brightly as ever, they were bouncing along at a considerable altitude. The scenery about was as bare as Bodmin Moor. Nothing flourished.

For all his anxieties for his son and, in a measure, for his wife and himself, Langstreet's spirits were high. He clutched the shotgun with which he had been issued. He felt in these barren spaces some correspondence with his innermost feelings. It seemed to him that, just as the greatest narrative works leave the impression that nothing worth considering has been overlooked, so a cycle of his life was in the act of being completed: not only was he now traversing a land with allies who had once been his despised father's enemies, but, in a contrary fashion, he was justifying his German origins by entering a danger zone to rescue his son.

So he said to Kathi, with a gesture to the wilderness outside the car, 'You don't wonder these poor people are so poor...'

'Or so hard,' she said.

The Iron Jelloid turned his mighty head to say, 'Crete is a favoured land for holidaymakers. But for us who live here, whose bare lives are filled with hot Cretan air, we have a position between Europe and Africa, which presents a difficulty. Things are taken from us by geography.'

'What –' began Langstreet, but Kathi nudged him into silence.

She needed silence, being filled with contradictory impulses. She was excited by what might possibly happen; she was appalled to be trapped in this crisis. Also, she felt some anxiety regarding her husband, whose normal, rather meticulous and painstaking way through life had given place to what she saw as a carefree cowboy attitude to their adventure. She knew this just by the way he clutched the gun in his lap.

And she wondered if there were old temptations, something inherited, over which he had triumphed but which still retained their potency.

Maderakis was muttering as if hypnotised. 'Ascent is being made to the grand scale. You find no signposts, tavernas, or no toilets towards these heights. We must be soon at Frasas. Later rise the White Mountains of fable, so bleak they are legends, where the world becomes only stone. You certainly don't laugh at them...'

The line of three vehicles was now climbing in low gear. The police became more alert. They approached a junction. What might be considered the main road led downwards to a valley. It was labelled with a pointed sign: FRASAS. The convoy took the right fork, whereupon the surface deteriorated.

Grinding slowly along, they reached an eminence, where Nikolis Fraghiadakis, in the lead vehicle, signalled for them to stop. He jumped out of the car, looking vigorous, warning them to be silent. The men all climbed out, clutching their weapons. Kathi followed, registering the scene with interest.

She stood watching by the lead car. The men, all but Maderakis, got down on their hands and knees to crawl to a point where the hill fell away. Not so far below them, a number of huts and other buildings clustered. A church was prominent, standing at the end of a short street. Two vehicles were parked by the church, diminished by distance.

Both Fraghiadakis and Maderakis brought binoculars into play, studying the layout of Frasas, looking for movement.

'Nothing moving down there,' said Fraghiadakis, quietly. 'Looks like they're holed up in the church.'

'Or the house next to the church,' corrected Tsouderakis, coming up to them. He had not enjoyed being outranked by the other. 'Keep your voices down – sound carries up here. Yiannis is our best sniper. He will stay here, and will cover our movements. We will drive down and take them by surprise.'

'They will hear our engines.'

'We drive to the road junction, then walk.'

He turned briskly and summoned Yiannis. Yiannis came up smartly, carrying his carbine. Tsouderakis positioned him at the peak of the hill, where he could have command of the whole village. 'Any problems, shoot!' was Tsouderakis' order.

At the road junction, leaving the vehicles, they set off briskly on foot, with Archie and Kathi bringing up the rear. Total silence prevailed round about. The sun shone high in a cloudless bowl of blue.

It had seemed at first to the two foreigners that Frasas represented an oasis of habitation in a waste of nothingness. As they neared the cluster of buildings, this impression faded before reality. The buildings and their outhouses had long been deserted. Dogs, cats, hens, rats, had taken over from humans. The hens that survived had rediscovered the art of flight.

The vacant homes were skeletal. Their tiles had, in many cases, been blown away in gales. Their doors had been ripped off by itinerants looking for firewood. Their walls had fallen in. The trees planted in the street – there was but one street – had overgrown their welcome, while some had overcome the buildings before which they stood. By the ceaseless activity of worms and things underground, such paving as there was had become uneven. It was safer to walk in the middle of the street.

When the contingent reached the first house, they huddled to discuss their plan of attack. Those who had looked merely cheerful on the walk from the vehicles now looked grim, and held their carbines close to their chests. Tsouderakis glanced up at the hill to check on Yiannis' position.

'We don't want shooting if it can be helped,' said Tsouderakis. 'These fellows are not killers, nor are we. They're amateurs. It is not a war. They'll give up at the sight of a gun.'

Captain Maderakis divided the bunch into two. One bunch to move forward behind the houses on one side of the street, one on the other. Kathi to stay behind, safe where she was. She made no protest. Archie nodded his thanks. As the others dispersed, she simply stood in the shadow of the first house, peeping round the corner at the empty street, where a hen wandered, pecking the dust.

Langstreet went with Tsouderakis and one of the police. They reached the vicinity of the church without trouble, to cluster behind the house next to the church. From the far side of the road, Maderakis signalled that he and his men were in place.

Maderakis fired a shot in the air, and shouted in Greek for the criminals to show themselves.

When the echoes of the shot died away, silence fell.

Maderakis fired a second shot.

A man came running from the side door of the house. Tsouderakis stepped forward smartly, gun levelled, shouting to him to halt. The man stopped at once and raised his hands above his head. The police officer came forward and put handcuffs on him. Langstreet guarded him, pinning him against a wall with the mule of his rifle. He was a poor specimen, thin and dirty, wearing torn jeans and a bandanna round his head to keep his long, greasy hair in place.

In a minute, another man was rounded up, a tough and intelligent-looking man, angry and shouting threats in Greek. He also was handcuffed, and tied with a length of rope to the first prisoner. Neither prisoner was threatened with any violence once they were secured. Tsouderakis spoke to them in quite a friendly way.

He then entered the house in which the gang members had been sheltering.

103

The other police stood with their guns ready, aimed at the windows and door. A third member of the gang emerged, hands raised above his head. He was aged and downcast. Maderakis took charge of him, handcuffing him to the other two prisoners. In response to the man's pleas, he gave him a cigarette, a Carter.

Shortly afterwards, Tsouderakis brought out a dazed-looking Clifford, having untied his legs and hands. He had found Langstreet's son bound to a chair and otherwise unharmed. A cheer went up at his appearance. Langstreet burst forward and embraced his son. Tears ran down his cheeks.

As they walked back down the deserted street with their prisoners, Tsouderakis said cheerfully to Langstreet, 'You see, that is how we like it to be – no bloodshed. These are really not bad men, only desperate because of no work to be had. So you have a bad image.'

Langstreet was weeping with relief as he hugged his son, and did not reply.

'There were four in the gang. One is missing,' said Maderakis, looking vaguely about him. He directed one of his men to inspect the church. Fraghiadakis, meanwhile, entered the house in which Clifford had been detained, emerging later in triumph, carrying the typewriter stolen long ago from the garage in Kyriotisa.

Langstreet's arm was about his son's shoulder. For once the rather grim lines of his face had relaxed, as if the pain of being human had been remitted.

'Justice is done, our honour is saved!' exclaimed Fraghiadakis. 'Let's get out of here. It's a good day's work, boys!'

Kathi, still waiting at the corner of a deserted house, felt steel at her throat. A low voice growled something in Greek. Presumably it told her not to move. She was unable to move in any case. She had become frozen with shock. She remained motionless as a hand, hard and rough, came over her shoulder and began to feel her for weapons. The knife remained at her throat as the hand travelled across her breasts, then lower, round her hips, between the crotch of her jeans. It paused there, came up, fumbled at her belt, then dug down into her panties. When the hand was withdrawn, she heard its owner sniffing at it.

All this took little time. The hand had moved fast. She was spun around, to look up into a young, emaciated, beardless face. It gave a rictus of a smile, briefly revealing tarnished teeth. The youth had a scrubby shock of jet-black hair, evidently dyed, and tied into place by a yellow bandanna. The knife came away from Kathi's throat, and was transferred to her back. The point pierced her clothes and dug into her flesh. When she gave a shriek of pain, the hand that had explored her came up and struck her in the face.

The youth then prodded her into action, holding tightly to her upper arm. He moved backwards, in part facing her, in part watching for the police. They were sheltered from sight by the ragged line of buildings. To their other side was the hill. She saw what he intended. She was his hostage, guaranteeing his safety; he was heading for the vehicles parked at the road junction, intent on making a getaway in one of them.

She dared not call out. It occurred to her that she might trip him, but feared to do so: she would have fallen with him. She hated this vile man, hatred now conquering fear because he had invaded her clothes. Thinking ahead, she tried to plan how she might slam the door of the truck on his legs as he climbed into the driving seat – if she was given the chance. Or maybe there was a loaded police revolver in the front locker...

The youth moved fast, still part-dragging her, still keeping a wary eye on the line of buildings they were leaving behind.

They were out in the open now. He turned and began to run towards the parked vehicles, pulling Kathi with him by the arm. It was at this point that his head burst apart. The sound of a shot followed. The black scalp and yellow bandanna flew as a unit, disintegrating as it went. He ran another pace, releasing his grasp on Kathi, then fell to his knees. He sprawled full length on the ground. She stood for a moment, splashed in his blood, hands up to her face. When her legs gave way, she collapsed, close to the ruined body.

Yiannis the sniper came down from his eyrie on the hill, looking extremely pleased with himself. Nearing Kathi, he raised a finger. 'One shot!' he said. 'Very good one shot.'

Langstreet and his son were approaching with the police. When Langstreet saw his wife on the ground, he ran to her aid.

This is presumably what Percy Shelley was on about when he said, 'We want the imaginative faculty to imagine that which we know'. He also called the imagination 'the great instrument of moral good'.

Much of the enjoyment of fiction derives from our unconscious reading of it. The events at Frasas will be interpreted according to temperament – our temperaments having been in part moulded by experience. On the surface, the events just related are moderately shocking. Yet, to stress the positive side of the matter, they depict a father's love for his son and, in the final sentence, his love for his wife. They show the police behaving sensibly and mercifully to enforce the law.

On the negative side, we have the horrific business of a young man's dying. We also see the effect it may have on Kathi's life (a neglect to which she drew attention earlier in the story). One root cause of these events is the poverty of this part of Crete, of which we shall hear more later (if I ever finish this novel before being arrested on trumped-up sex charges).

The trick we perform is to strike a balance between positives and negatives. Thus our judgements become developed. We may be aware of none of this while we read; but we are operating on Shelley's principle, and imagining, putting into imaginative form, that which we know: that death is bad, love is good.

Our unconscious minds work fast in picking up all such elements while, at the same time, our rational minds continue reading the surface of the story. So we can have it both ways. This episode shows the police in a more favourable light than hitherto. We 'naturally' identify with law and order. But surely we also identify to some extent with the criminals. These lawless elements, living in the wild, half-starved, have a background of misery and depravation, brought about in part by war. Does not some fragment of our overfed selves admire them? An admiration prompted here by the puny triumph of the police in recovering a worn typewriter, stolen long since? 'There ain't,' as I remember a woman once said, in an otherwise forgotten B-movie, 'no justice'.

But what, you may well ask, what about the writer's mind?

I can't claim control over my unconscious mind. It moves in a mysterious way, its wonders to perform (i.e. in earning me my livelihood as a writer). Yet I see here my sympathy for women; a sympathy so often set aside by other men where men's interests are concerned. And of course there's the desolation of Frasas, the ruinous village, to be considered. My novels (*New Investments* is an example) are rarely set amid sumptuous surroundings, where the prosperous live and move. Mine is the literature of the underdog, hence my sympathy for the underbitch: woman. My deserted village is a symbol of the desertions that afflicted my early life.

In a way, my later life has been just as bad. But more fun.

A writer's life has its consolations, for all that reviewers and critics can do or say. You can give your unconscious a good gallop now and then.

Back in Geneva, Archie Langstreet immediately took his wife and son to church, to offer thanks to God for their safe deliverance. Afterwards, as they stood in the shadow of the church, awaiting their car, Langstreet remarked to his wife that she had seemed, as he put it, unenthusiastic.

'If we give thanks to God for deliverance from a nasty mess,' said Kathi, smiling at him, 'have we not the right to blame him for getting us into the mess?'

'Kathi, that is not the way of Faith.'

Their car arrived, their chauffeur apologising for lateness, owing to the dense traffic. Once they were in their seats, the vehicle wound its way through the great roaring city and up to the Vielle Ville, where their apartment was situated, looking over a leafy part of the city. Caryatids guarded their doorway.

As the manservant presented Langstreet with his post, the phone rang. Langstreet was tossing junk mail away when his secretary announced that the local TV station hoped to interview him and his son on the day's *Newsnight*.

'I'll speak to them, Dad,' Cliff said. 'Do you want to do it?'

'No. It may sound as if I am criticising the Cretans. You go, Cliff. It was your adventure.'

Langstreet nodded to Kathi, as if he had gained her assent, and hurried after his secretary into his study. Kathi stood where she was, uncertainly, and then walked slowly into the living room. She walked among the expensive Second Empire furniture, collected assiduously in French sale rooms; it, and the statuary enclosed in glass cabinets, were not greatly to her taste. Nor, she suspected, to Archie's, since his religious conversion.

She went to the windows in their deep embrasures and stared out at a row of plane trees, still in the quiet afternoon. She steadied herself with her fingers on the sill. She was trembling.

She had trembled ever since the incident at Frasas. Although she had meekly accompanied her husband to church, the service had not helped her.

At length, with a gesture of impatience, she turned away and went into the main bedroom, where she began slowly to unpack her suitcase. Her actions were somewhat lackadaisical. After that, she rang for the maid and asked for coffee. When coffee arrived on a silver tray, she did not at first attempt to pour the liquid; instead, she went to her husband's study, to look in at him.

He turned a serious face towards her. It dissolved at once into a smile. The secretary too looked up and smiled, then turned back to her computer. He said, 'Darling, I'm afraid I'm going to be rather entangled with the law case for the next month. We have to pin down Nentelstam while we have the chance. Can't let them get away.'

'Of course.' She smiled back at him. 'Call me if there's anything I can do. Would you like some coffee?'

'Renate will get us some when we need it.'

'I'm feeling terribly upset, by the way.'

'Of course, of course. It was upsetting.'

Kathi retreated. At nine that evening, she called Langstreet to watch the TV interview with Clifford.

At one point, the interviewer said, 'Obviously, you must have been aware that there was some danger involved in visiting Crete, in which your grandfather had been notoriously active.'

Clifford was pale but composed. 'Although I knew that my grandfather had been part of the invasion of Crete, it was hardly in the forefront of my mind. Why should it have been? Whatever he did, it was nothing to do with me. And Crete is a peaceful and pleasant place.'

'It obviously wasn't very peaceful where you were concerned.'

'The men who captured me did not harm me. They made it clear that I was a decoy. It was my father – who is as innocent as I – they were after. My relations with these men was, on the whole, good.'

'Nevertheless, in the rescue operation, one of them was shot. Wasn't that the case?'

'That was rather different. He was young and foolish. He had a knife at my stepmother's throat.'

'Obviously you will not wish to return to Crete after this experience, will you?'

'Possibly not. But the background to what happened is that that part of Crete is very poor. It's a pleasant area, nevertheless, full of interesting Byzantine churches. They rely on tourism. No one should be put off making a visit by what happened to me.'

'You're saying, however, that obviously you and your family won't return there?'

'Well, not for a while...'

'Thank you, Clifford Langstreet.'

When Cliff returned to the apartment, his father clapped him on the shoulder, telling him he spoke well. Kathi kissed him. She asked if he had enjoyed the interview.

Cliff said, 'Do you remember when the buzz-word was "clearly"? Now the interviewers prefer "obviously".'

At which point, the phone rang. It was Vibe to speak to Cliff.

'Ask her to join us here,' Kathi said, quickly.

But Vibe had a job in Stockholm. She could not manage to visit Switzerland because she had to work. Everyone, it seemed, had to work. Cliff flew back to England to his administrative job in Coutts' bank. Archie was in court every day, following the progress of the WHO's lawsuit against Nentelstam, and working hard in his study by night.

Kathi, at a loss, took coffee with her friends in the morning, visited the cinema in the afternoon, and wept in the evening.

Chapter Six

I took the opportunity to speak to Kathi myself. By this time I had shed my annoying false moustache.

'Kathi, I have been writing about you for some while, yet I really do not know the sort of woman you are. You are brave, yes, sensible, sensuous; but what lies beneath those qualities I have no idea. At present, you are extremely upset, understandably.'

'Obviously. I don't feel inclined to talk, either.'

'Of course. But I'm not sure I understand the nature of your marriage to Archie, for instance. Can you tell me something about yourself?'

She reached for a cigarette and lit it. She sighed deeply.

'I suppose I can give you some facts regarding my upbringing, if you are interested. As to the nature of my marriage...Well... You often hear people saying that the nature of so-and-so's marriage is a mystery. Isn't that because the bond between two people is always something of a mystery – not least to the couple themselves? I have a great compassion for Archie. I see how he wants constantly to confirm his Englishness. Yet we live too rarely in our England houses. He lives much of his time here, in a German-speaking world.'

'You love him?'

'Of course. Obviously.' She smiled, self-consciously 'being interviewed'. She stubbed out the cigarette after two puffs.

'Does this contradiction annoy you in any way?'

'Oh, aren't we all full of contradictions? We may never resolve them. Accidents of birth – the period in which we were born… If you want to know something of my life, well, for a start, I was born in Hungary, into a rich Magyar-Jewish family. Or the family had been rich. The Second World War was a turning point for us, as it was for the Langenstrasses, though in a milder way.

'At least we escaped most of the pogroms. My father had influence. Besides, as you probably know, the destruction of Hungarian Jews was a pretty on-off-on affair, compared with the merciless treatment of them elsewhere. I mean the destruction, as opposed to the persecution… You may know that Hungarian Jewish communities survived intact until 1944. Then the fate of the Jews depended on whether the Prime Ministers were pro-Nazi or only reluctant collaborators. Even before that, definitions of what constituted Jewishness changed, because of the struggle between the Catholic Church and Germany.

'My father was in the wine trade, together with his brother and cousins. Others of the family were in the armaments business. Slowly, they were being disbarred from such professions, and so times became harder. Both my parents were arrested in July of 1944 and sent to a ghetto in the city of Szeged, where they died. Then that peasant boy's head being shot off…'

She shivered in horror, and clasped her hands between her knees.

'My uncle Antal saved me from death. He had rejected Judaism and married a Catholic woman with good connections. He managed to purchase train tickets by bribery for me, my aunt, and himself. So we arrived by terrific good fortune in the port of Trieste, after a three-day journey. At one point, we were saved from arrest only by a fortuitous Allied air raid, which occurred at the city of Zagreb, where we had to change trains. My memory of those times remains vivid.

'Uncle got us at last to Rome. If you remember, Italy had changed sides in the war, and now fought with the Allies against the Nazis. Everything was in a terrible muddle, but at least there was no more persecution of the Jews. We lived out the war in one room, a little attic room. I was fortunate in getting a part-time job in an art gallery. I honour my auntie, who could have remained safely in Budapest. But she loved uncle – and me. She took care of us.'

'No rows in that little attic room?' I asked.

'Oh, there were some, of course. "Obviously". Uncle Antal was distressed. He longed for news of the family, but most of them had died natural deaths, or were in hiding, or had been killed. It was very sad. After the war was over, Aunt Marie wanted to return to Hungary. Then we received news that mother and father had died of starvation and pneumonia in the Szeged ghetto. Uncle mourned the death of his beloved brother. Oh, how he cried. I couldn't bear to see and hear a grown man crying like that. So ugly! Only later did I believe that he cried for the whole world.

'I was by then adolescent. I couldn't stand uncle's grief! He refused to go back to Hungary. I backed him up in that, because I had met an Italian boy.

'I wanted to stop being a Jew, stop being Hungarian, stop all that, forget the past. I wanted to live.'

'You went to school in Rome? What was that like?'

'You mean racially? It was okay. There was a mixed bunch of kids, all nations. It was funded by the Catholic Church and run by nuns. I think I quite enjoyed that time, because there was no threat – none of the threats we had previously lived under.'

'What was your state of mind at that time?' I asked.

Kathi paused a moment, thinking, gazing down at the coffee table as if the past were embedded in it.

'No doubt I was what used to be called a "crazy mixed-up kid". But I think I was pretty happy. I lived in a world of change. We all did. Surrounding us was the excitement of Rome beginning to glitter again, to start a new life. Fashion shows, smart clothes, new cars, flashy science fiction magazines, strange movies – you remember Fellini's *La Strada*? Oh! – and cops in astonishing uniforms, gaudy shops with gaudy façades – all that sort of thing. Oh, and art. Not only the great Renaissance painters but also the Futurists and the new breed of poster artists. It was colourful, intense, sexy… I became promiscuous. Promiscuity meant being alive, being modern.'

'What did you get up to?'

Kathi smiled at me. 'I know something of *your* past. I know you're a dirty old man! I'm not telling. Except that I jumped into bed with other girls as well as boys. I didn't care. Later, I became ashamed of the things I got up to.'

'That was after you met the Reverend Archie, I suppose.'

Her look seemed to blend sauciness and sarcasm. 'Sex is a bit of a mystery, isn't it? Isn't that why you still keep on writing about it, despite your age?'

I put a finger to my head and shot myself with it. 'Touché!'

'I think I fell for Archie because he was so clearly a good, moral man. And my opinion of myself was not good.'

She lapsed into a silence, musing, which I did not disturb. She now seemed almost happy, talking about her Italian past. I saw how well her dress fitted her, the fabric tight and firm over her bosom, looser about her throat. She appeared at ease within the garment, just as I had always seen her at ease within her life.

'How did you come to meet Archie?'

'As I believe I told you, my uncle had been a wine merchant in Budapest, on quite a grand scale. He picked up the trade again in Rome. He met an English army officer in the Intelligence Corps, a man named Graham Flower. Flower had money. Between them, they created a trade in Chianti with the UK. The English had been starved of wine during the war. They bought Antal-Flower Chianti by the shipload. It seemed they couldn't get enough Chianti in those post-bellum years.

'Soon, uncle and Flower were able to buy their own ship, an old tramp steamer, which for some years shipped all the wine to England. It was on that ship I came to England.'

'You and your aunt?'

Kathi looked sorrowful. 'Auntie Marie stayed in Rome. She could not face the cold and wet of England, she said. Of course, with global warming, it hasn't been too bad in recent years. She became an artists' model and later married one of the artists. We still keep in touch. I see her once a year, either in Rome or by the lakes. Como is our favourite lake. It's still so pretty.'

'So what happened then? After you got to England?'

'I didn't like London at first. Then I got a job in a firm of lawyers and there I met Archie. He was kind to me – kind and scrupulous. He was married. Married to a rather bitchy Englishwoman, a woman called Rosemary. But Archie and I had something in common. A big thing. We were both displaced persons.'

I laughed. 'Displaced but adaptable. I suppose you have to be. What happened then?'

'Through Archie I got to know England well. The south coast, the Cotswolds…'

'You *like* the Cotswolds?!'

She paused and looked at me, smiling quizzically.

'Why are you interested in all this? You listen so patiently. You're not displaced.'

'In a way I am. My father was in foreign service. He was with the British Embassy staff in Manilla when I was born. Mother was interested only in the social life. She was American. I was brought up by a Polynesian nursemaid. My parents used to dump me on her when they flew back to England for leave. I resented that bitterly. So I consider myself deserted. Several times deserted. Somehow, I've never fitted into English life. But let's hear more about you, Kathi. Archie divorced Rosemary and married you – how long did that take?'

'Divorce wasn't so easy in those days… Anyhow, at last he was free. So was Rosemary. She got massive damages off poor Archie. Took all his Matisses. All she left him with was a set of novels by a terrible sporting writer called… Er, not Striptease – Surtees.'

'Surtees? Never heard of him.'

'Almost directly after the *decree nisi*, she went off and married a member of the so-called aristocracy, Basil Fanthorpe de Vere.'

'Good God,' I said. 'I know Rosemary de Vere. Met her in Greece.'

She gave me a searching look.

'Really? Did you like her?'

'As a matter of fact – I shouldn't tell you this – I shat on her.'

We both burst into peals of laughter.

'Obviously,' Kathi said.

And then (all narratives contain 'and thens') the ikon arrived from Agios Ioannis, well fortified with bubble wrap and cardboard. Kathi unwrapped it with care. She took the precious thing over to the window to study it.

The immaculate stasis of the painting penetrated her. Austere Agia Anna cradled the infant Christ with her head slightly to one side, as if in submission to a will greater than hers. Age was indicated – hinted at – by shadows under Anna's eyes, the shades mortality brings, as early indicators of its intentions. With her left arm and hand she steadied the babe, while her right, with its long fingers, steadied her modest teat, barely revealed in its freedom from her gown. This gown was rendered in a dull brick-red. Its folds were painstakingly depicted. The infant Christ was wrapped like a cocoon in swaddling bands. The babe gazed up contentedly at Anna. Both figures were haloed. They stood out from the golden background, representing heaven. Monaché Kostas had worked well, secure in the depths of the Mesovrahi Gorge.

A tear ran down Kathi's cheek. The religious symbolism meant little to her. It was the trust and dependency of the child which touched her. Archie had not wished for a child by her. His career had come first.

Gaining this ikon had been paid for by her presiding nightmare. Again and again, the youth abducting her had his head blown off in her face. The splatter of blood and jelly remained to taint her mind. Yet here was the babe before her, sinless...

Kathi carried the ikon into Langstreet's study. Langstreet sat at his desk, examining it carefully. He took a magnifying glass from a drawer to pursue the detail before looking up at Kathi.

'Yes, it is of excellent quality. A real original!'

'But, Archie, it is actually a forgery, isn't it?'

He made a slight dismissive gesture. 'There's not another ikon of Agia Anna suckling Jesus extant, is there?'

She had to admit it was true. She had communicated on the internet with churches in Greece, Romania, Bulgaria and Turkey. No one admitted knowledge of such an ikon.

'Now we have it, are we going to use it?' she asked.

'Use it? We'll see. Thank you for showing it to me. What do you want us to do with it? Send your monk some dollars, will you? I must study this batch of papers.' He indicated the muddle before him on the desk. 'Tomorrow, Nentelstam plans to bring in witnesses to support the quality of their product.'

The Nentelstam Corporation had engaged a raft of able lawyers, chief among whom was the chubby-cheeked and seemingly amiable Günter Schlechter. Schlechter was a master of obfuscation. Every day, he brought to court a fresh set of statistics which proved that the products of the Nentelstam Corporation brought benefit and joy wherever they were purchased. Schlechter called into question the findings of the World Health Organisation, and of small lobbying groups such as Baby Milk Action.

Over the ensuing months, the trial consisted of complex evidence, brought forward by both sides, for and against the correct formulae for commercial infant milks. Research had indicated that infants who were not breast-fed required long-chain polyunsaturated fatty acids such as were present in cod liver oil. The extent to which such LCPUFA assisted the development of visual and brain tissue was the subject of heated debate. So the hearings dragged on.

Kathi could not endure the protracted battle. She returned alone to England, to the Langstreet apartment in Kensington. There she sought counselling from an old psychiatrist friend, Lulu Geismar. She was a resilient woman. Gradually the nightmare of Frasas faded. (But still the trial in Geneva continued.)

Günter Schlechter claimed that no statistically significant research had been done on the subject of infant intelligence. He rejected out of hand the claim that the Corporation put pressure on mothers in the Third World to abandon breast-feeding in preference for their formula milks, in order to boost their enormous profits. The Corporation simply met demand with supply; they advertised in competition with rival companies. For many mothers in difficulties – many cases were adduced – Nentelstam's milk formulae proved essential, and saved many lives.

The tide of evidence began to turn against the prosecution.

Langstreet, the man who had brought the case – the culmination of his term of office in WHO – sat at the back of the courtroom every day, and every night went over the next day's presentation with his legal team. He was swallowed up by the proceedings.

His wife, however, pursued a different objective, the one the tabloid newspapers called 'The Case of the Cretan Teat'. Kathi had recovered her fighting spirit. Armed with faithful colour reproductions of the ikon, she approached the leading art magazines in Germany, France, Britain, Holland and the USA. Within the folder containing the artwork went a brief article describing the discovery of this beautiful lost religious work, and its startling significance.

In every case, the story was taken up, although published results were slow to appear. However, Kathi (aided by her secretary) sent out a second and larger wave of colour reproductions. Accompanying these went an article stressing a different aspect of the story. This article stressed the poverty of Crete, where the ikon had been discovered in a practically derelict chapel in an olive grove. It suggested that the story of the grandmother suckling the infant Jesus should be better known, in particular because it demonstrated the unity of the Holy Family.

This wave of submissions went out to leading television companies all around the world, to leading newspapers, and to Catholic journals.

Kathi presented a third wave of reproductions and articles to ecologists and green parties everywhere, and to such groups as Baby Milk Action. Here the article was brief, and suggested that the slogan 'Jesus Enjoyed Breast Milk' would be neither blasphemous nor inappropriate.

The results were more than she could have anticipated. Europe and the United States and those other countries (Japan, for instance) which comprise what is known as the 'Western World' were at this period untroubled by any matters other than the drunken antics of certain footballers, a few gruesome murders distributed equally among the nations, speculations on the sex life of a prominent Head of State, the crisis in Nicaragua, the cloning of a Rottweiler in Finland, the attempts of a man and a pet gorilla to circumnavigate the world in a hot-air balloon, the ever-increasing destitution of the Third World, and such trivia. Into this vacuum, the Cretan Teat dropped like a tactical nuclear weapon into a stagnant pond.

The remarkable revelation – to some religious, to others merely hilarious – of Saint Anna's breast in Christ's mouth provoked a sensation on many levels. An issue of *Der Sturm* reproduced the ikon on its front page, under the headline 'JESUS SUCKS!' It was withdrawn, following protests from the Vatican.

A headline 'GRAN CAN!' proved more acceptable. Many French TV stations showed an array of breasts from the developing world, which evolved into a popular Internet guessing game, 'Beat the Teat – which was the Virgin Mary's?'

Such frivolity was widely deplored. Questions were debated, such as why Anna's grandmotherly assistance was necessary; why the important fact of her assistance was omitted from the Gospels; and why the Blessed Virgin Mary's milk had dried up: could it be because of the irregularity of the conception? The Second Century *Protovangelium* of James was retranslated and reprinted in all European languages, to become a bestseller in most of them. From the reproduction of the ikon on its covers, the Langstreets received royalties.

The feast of St Anna had been observed in the tenth century in Naples. It was revived there with great ceremony. Canada, too, hotted up the Feast Day on 26th July. Breast-shaped pasties, stuffed with chopped lamb, went on sale in New York and elsewhere; initially called 'Anne Treats', they soon became famous as 'Annetits'. Well, what do you expect?

The Third World, in its less amusing way, also took to the ikon, where its significance was not lost on downtrodden motherhood.

But it was in Greece that the ikon had its greatest impact, as we shall see.

The day came when Kathi received a not unexpected phone call from Geneva. The WHO case had failed. Kathi was enjoying life. Every day, something fresh regarding Agia Anna came in, and more coverage arrived at her desk. She sent a large donation to Monaché Kostas. She engaged a staff of three to handle the traffic. She found she enjoyed appearing on TV news and arts programmes.

But upon receiving the call, she packed a bag and flew to Archie's side in their apartment in the Vielle Ville.

Archie Langstreet wept unrestrainedly in his wife's arms... The evidence against the Corporation, in the judgement of the presiding judge, had not proved conclusive. The sale of infant milk formulae by the Nentelstam Corporation could not be proved directly to harm babies; too many other factors were involved. The milk substitute was of benefit to those mothers whose own milk had dried. 'Not all mothers,' noted the judge, with a predictable attempt at topicality, 'could rely on their mothers to provide, as we now know the Blessed Virgin Mary was able to do.'

Kathi held her husband till his grief abated. Finally, he took out a white handkerchief and wiped his eyes.

'Apologies, dear Kathi. A moment of weakness. To think that that wretched corporation should be awarded damages! After all the years of work… It's hard to take.'

'You've done your best, darling. They had lawyers like Schlechter on their side.'

'I'm so ashamed to think that the WHO will have to pay up. And UNICEF… And I shall retire under a cloud, disgraced.'

He broke into a fresh attack of weeping. Kathi held him in her arms, kissing his forehead.

'It's a natural reaction, my love. You have worked so hard. You are exhausted.' She stroked his head tenderly.

He looked with affection into her eyes. 'Everything is part of a Greater Design. We must see the Lord's hand in this. I cannot despair or turn away. Something more is required of me. He needs me to work his will.'

Kathi tutted. 'Let the Lord manage without you! His purposes will take a long time to work out; they're so complicated, so bloody complicated. You should take it easy now.'

With a flash of spirit, he replied, 'I cannot take it easy. If I have failed here, then I must succeed elsewhere. It is God's will. I know it is required of me.'

She sighed and said that she would order the maid to make them some coffee.

To work effectively, a novel has to have some significance, to cast a light, a glow, or maybe a shadow, beyond its narrative, after its conclusion. So I used to say, to sound a bit grand, when interviewed on TV.

Yet in a way I believe it to be true. If only it applied to my novels! How wonderful to write like A S Byatt – real 'literary fiction'! We should not just pass through a novel; it ought to pass through us, the way figs do. It doesn't matter if we don't enjoy it much. Then we can contemplate it afterwards and possibly be changed by it, if we can see it whole, embodying something fragrant with wisdom, or something hitherto unperceived: though I know I should not be saying this – and would not be, were it not for Henry Fielding.

(But note that my sentences are beginning to twist and entangle as recommended by Virginia Woolf, so you can't say I'm anti-feminist.)

The means of achieving this degree of perfection is to sustain an illusion that we are talking about a real three-dimensional world that meets the demands of what we regard as psychologi-cally acceptable – while at the same time satisfying our wish to be surprised. So we suspend disbelief while we read. Oh, I know well enough how to do the trick, even if I don't always carry it off. But we must remain to some extent aware that we are suspending our disbelief. As I was finding with *The Victor Hugo Club*. Much of the pleasure lies in enjoying make-believe.

So you think all this expanse of pages is make-believe? You think I spoil the make-believe by strutting about in my own fiction? Then let me tell you this: I have the very ikon, the ikon that Monaché Kostas painted, hanging right here on the wall of my study.

Reader, I commissioned him!

Pandering to your wish to be surprised, I may say I am able to talk about literature while resting with Ingrid beside me, in a small hotel in Kastrup. You remember Ingrid? She and I met in Paleohora. Since I had failed to climb onto her balcony, she cannot have had very high hopes for me. Nevertheless, being of an amiable nature, she invited me to stay with her in Kastrup, a pleasant town near the Copenhagen airport.

Her invitation came just in time. I had given up on the Cotswolds and my false moustache, and returned to my flat in London. My finances were at a low ebb. In the late seventies, I had had great success with *From the Enchanter Fleeing*. But the royalties had slowly dwindled, and none of my books since then had met with the same acclaim.

Which does not mean that they were no good. It's all a matter of pot luck. What do you expect?

In the chapter of *The Victor Hugo Club* I was reading, mention is made of the great fortunes amassed by many of the painters of the Renaissance. Raphael, for instance, left on his death a house in Urbino, together with a palace, vineyards, and land near Rome, after a life led in luxury and splendour. Here was I, behind with the rent on my apartment and, like Rembrandt, long past the zenith of renown.

Fortunately, I am of a cheerful disposition, and would not have changed my life with anyone. Though I would not have minded being a woman for a day, to find out some of their secrets.

Pushing open the door of my flat, I found threatening letters from solicitors who were lying in wait for me.

More cheering was a letter from Boris on lined notepaper. He had settled down on a smallholding in a Norfolk village called Upwell. He was radiantly happy. With him was his partner, Robin. Robin was good with pigs.

I had my forebodings about this. There was the name of the village, for one thing. I rang the number he gave me. After a long wait, a woman's voice answered. 'Robin here,' she said. So that was okay. Evidently his problem with premature ejaculation in the days of Lucia had not soured his relations with the female sex. When you are a kid, the first experience of getting it in is so exciting that you immediately yield an offering to whatever gods there be. After all, what do you expect?

The very next morning, while I was still in bed, the doorbell rang. I flung on a dressing-gown and went to see who it was.

It was the postman. He made me sign for a registered letter from Sylvia Beltrau's lawyers. The letter summoned me to appear at Number Two Court in the Old Bailey, on such-and-such a date, a week ahead.

'Bugger!' I said.

Providentially, there was this other letter from Denmark, my address written in Ingrid's elegant hand.

After showering, I dressed, grabbed a cup of coffee, and went to see the nearest travel agent. At least I had the price of a flight. Or rather, I charged it to my Visa card.

Ingrid met me at Kastrup airport. She was a pleasantly sturdy figure of medium height, with dark eyes set behind her high rosy cheeks. She was an unusual-looking woman of considerable beauty; a well-preserved fifty-five, I thought. The glow of seeing her again was somewhat diminished by the presence of her daughter, Lisa. Ingrid kissed me affectionately and we bundled into her small car.

'What happened about that funny wall-painting you found, darling?' Ingrid asked, as we drove along. I liked the 'darling'. 'The woman with her little tits feeding baby Jesus Christ? I told so many people about that painting. Everyone laughs always. It must have been a forgery, don't you think?'

'I hope not! I am writing a novel about it.'

'Oh, yes, of course, you are a writer. I had forgotten. You wrote such a nice letter to me. How can you imagine the life of that woman, Jesus' granny? Is anything known about her? Are you then a Roman Catholic?'

'The novel's not about her.'

'No? That's disappointing. You must tell us all about it. My husband will be interested.'

Her husband? I hadn't come all this way just to interest her bloody husband in my novel!

'I don't want to be a burden to you, Ingrid. I can put up at a nearby hotel.'

'No way. You are our guest. Sven wants to talk with you. We have a nice summerhouse where you can stay.' The car swerved wildly as she flashed a smile at me. Oh, that smile! Suddenly, I remembered it, and all my doubts faded away. That smile, those parted lips, those white teeth: together they were like a beaker full of the warm north. Yet they were flavoured with something less confident than the lady perhaps intended to convey, something pleading? Or apologetic? Its beauty and mystery, the secrecy behind its openness, invited one to know Ingrid better.

We turned down a side street, and then into a more open one, where small shops clustered and people strolled about in a leisurely way. Ingrid turned the car into a car park. We climbed out.

'It's all pedestrians here,' said Lisa. We walked up a side avenue and turned into a close, where apartment blocks were mixed with small scale housing. Number nine was where Ingrid lived.

From a narrow hallway, we went into a large open room which was living-room and kitchen, with a lot of chrome and blonde wood on view. A sister of Lisa's appeared, looking like a miniature version of Ingrid, but with dark hair. Ignoring her, Ingrid poured us two vodkas saying, as she handed me my glass, 'I don't suppose you want to be English and have tea, do you?'

We sat and chatted. Sven was nowhere to be seen. He kept irregular hours in a nearby electronics firm. He was working on a new semi-conductor.

The younger child was standing gazing at us.

'Dotta, can't you find something to do? Where's Sigbrit? Why don't you go and do one of your lovely mazes?'

The child, thus dismissed, moved away without leaving the room.

'It's their holidays,' said Ingrid. She sighed. 'Come on, I'll show you my artist's studio where I work when I'm not teaching.'

We climbed two flights of stairs to a fine light room under the roof, with windows front and rear. Ingrid's bright blobby paintings were ranged round the walls at ground level. I paid them some attention while checking the view from the windows. The south-facing window, looking away from the close, revealed a small, neat, paved garden with a summerhouse and a garage at the end of it. A rather faint road, resembling to my eyes a hedgeless English country lane, led from the garage away across country.

'It's yet quite a nice open view,' said Ingrid. She came up to me and put an arm round my waist. 'Of course it's not like Greece, but one might be happy here. If only… I am so miserable, though I seek not to show it. I have such anxiety. I must tell you, that my bloody husband has done – '

At that moment, the third of Ingrid's children, Sigbrit, a slightly smaller version of Dorothea, appeared. She wore a shirt and socks and nothing between.

'Mama, I can't find my jeans. I know – '

Ingrid rounded on her. 'You are not to walk about like that! How many times do you have to be told? Really, you'll have to be – '

She disappeared from the room, driving the child ahead of her. I stood at the window, feeling uncomfortable in the midst of this unsought domesticity, and disappointed, because any display of animosity towards Sven worked on my behalf in my role as female-comforter – I wished to hear more. Also, Ingrid had seemed so calm in Paleohora; here in her own house she appeared slightly neurotic. I thought of the great tribe of women, so attractive in the main to look at, so obliging in the main to be with, and yet – what folly to pursue a particular one of the tribe. They lived their own busy lives under their own laws; looking after, dressing, feeding, the dumb progeny their males had fathered on them. How could sex possibly be so constantly on their minds as on male minds? What do you expect?

Really, I would have been better off hiding out at home, continuing the story of Archie Langstreet's increasing obsession, and letting Ingrid sort out her own problems.

When I went downstairs, Ingrid was by the hotplate, cooking fish fingers in olive oil for her girls. A radio was playing cool jazz too loudly. I thought how neat her behind looked in her jeans.

The three girls were huddling together by their computer, tracing a maze on the monitor. This was achieved with plenty of shrieking, laughing, jostling, and shouts of 'That's not fair!'

'Do you want a fish finger?' Ingrid asked. 'We can have some Chardonnay to help wash it downwards.'

As I was pouring two glasses of Chardonnay, she said, 'My brother Jannick has his birthday today. We will go to his party tonight to celebrate. It's not far off. I think you will like that, will you?'

When I glanced enquiringly at the girls, she said, 'They think their Uncle Jannick is too strict. They will stay here and Kisa will look after them. Sven can come later if he would like. I'll leave him a note to remind him. We two will go alone at eight in the car.'

'Sounds good.'

Before we left, she escorted me down the garden to the summer-house, which proved better equipped than anticipated. I took a shower and changed my clothes for the evening.

In the car at eight, she said, 'You are not too pleased, are you? Did you expect me to be alone? When we were down in Paleohora, then I was alone. I threatened to divorce Sven. The little kids stayed with Jannick and Jannick's wife. I don't know why I do not leave Sven for good. He's a Swede, you know. I made a big big mistake there. He earns good money, but it goes to drink and women. And he did a vile thing. If I was on my own, I could work more and earn enough to survive, just about. But the girls need so much money. So I stay with Sven for security. The pig! God, I hate him. Fortunately, sex is quite good with him.'

I was sorry to hear that, but merely asked, 'What vile thing did he do?'

127

As the car swerved round a corner, so it seemed did the course of her soliloquy. 'What I most like is to be penetrated from behind. I mean with the prick in the proper place where it belongs, but from behind, so that the man can hold my tits and rub my clitoris, while the prick goes right up inside of me. It's such a good feeling. I come almost at once. The other way round, facing – well, it's okay, but not quite the same, somehow. I read somewhere in an anatomy article that it was from behind that early peoples always did it. Maybe it came from our ancestry with the apes. Apes still do it from behind, I believe?'

'They have to look out for danger, even when on the job. So it is the best position for them. But since bedrooms were invented, and door locks, then we don't have to look out for danger, and can stare into each other's eyes instead. And we can take longer about it.'

She waggled a finger. 'But there may be danger if it's a case of adultery.' She added, reflectively, 'Of course, that's when we want to take longest about it.'

The road outside Jannick's house was full of cars. Ingrid simply wedged her car onto the pavement between two others, and we squeezed out. More squeezing was required to get into the house. Jannick had invited in all his neighbours as well as his relations. We pushed our way through a great babble of Danish issuing from grinning faces. We took glasses of champagne from a proffered tray, and plunged on.

Ingrid met some long-lost cousins and began talking to them.

I said, 'Excuse me,' as I stepped on the toe of one of a group standing just behind me.

'Oh, you are English!' she said, and burst into laughter. She was a buxom blonde, one of a group of four, who laughed with her. 'That's funny.'

'You speak English?' I asked, not entirely pleased.

'We all can speak English if we bother,' said one of the men, wearing a T-shirt with a map of the state of Maryland printed on it, and they laughed again.

I said to the woman who had spoken first, 'You are wasting your time with these guys. Come with me and have some witty conversation. I'm not drunk like them.'

'You are too old,' she said, looking not displeased.

'Not too old for some things.'

The man with the T-shirt advertising Maryland said something sharp in his native tongue. She answered something which must have been the local equivalent of 'balls', took my arm, and pushed with me through the crowd.

'Where did you come from? How are you here?' She was not particularly pretty. I explained I was a friend of Ingrid's, that we had met in Crete and so forth.

'It must seem bad to come to this place and find it full of drunken Danish people. I am from Jutland. You must become drunken yourself. Then it will not feel so bad. There's vodka. I know where.'

Music was playing, harsh rock 'n' roll. Suddenly it changed to something of an earlier period, sweeter and slower.

As she pushed our way into the kitchen, she said, 'It's Herb Alpert and the Tiwana Band. For Jannick. He likes them. It's his period. Maybe yours too?'

She poured us two generous jiggers of Absolut vodka. Beyond the kitchen was a conservatory, unlit, unoccupied. I took her in there, drained my glass, flung the empty onto a wicker chair, took her in my arms and began to dance with her.

'We don't dance this way no more.'

'Any more. See what you're missing.' I kissed her. She turned her face, so that my kiss landed on her cheek.

The guy with the Maryland T-shirt came in at this juncture and pulled the blonde away from me.

'I would hit you if you were not old,' he said, looking pretty offended.

'I was in the Commandos. You touch me and you're on the floor with a broken neck, sonny, okay?'

'She's my girlfriend.'

'Is she? Too bad. She told me she was sick of your company and your breath smelt bad, and being in bed with you was like being shagged by a camel.'

At this, the girl burst out laughing. She was still laughing – and giving me a wave – as they disappeared back into the rabble.

The vodka must have gone to my head. I went and poured myself another dose, sank back into the wicker chair in the gloom, and took the drink slowly.

Lights came on in the conservatory, other people milled about, paying me no attention. Music in the main rooms was noisier now. I roused when Ingrid stood over me, saying brightly, 'Darling, I'd like you to meet my husband, Sven Andersson.'

I rose and shook hands with a gaunt man of bony feature, whose hair was plastered flat across his skull.

He asked me what part of England I was from. My answer puzzled him. 'Salisbury? Salisbury? I been many times to England. Never heard of Sainsbury.'

'Salisbury.'

'Quite, quite. Somewhere to the north of Southampton, I imagine?'

'Most places are.'

'I mean to say Northampton. No, you're getting me confused. Is there a football team calling itself East Hampton?'

'Oh, stop this!' Ingrid exclaimed. 'What does it matter? You're plainly drunk, Sven. Come on, both of you. Supper is prepared.'

'But the question isn't answered…' Nor was his question ever answered.

A large table had been laid, aglow with candles, cutlery and silverware. We lost Sven, happily, as he took a diversion towards the bar. 'The bastard's pissed again,' said Ingrid, over her shoulder.

The meal consisted of a number of dainty courses, mainly fish, some hot, many cold. All were washed down with an excellent white wine. Conversations ran sporadically up and down the table. We sang 'Happy Birthday' to Jannick, after which Ingrid rose to her feet.

'I love you all! You are all lovely people. Also you are intelligent – with a few exceptions. So I beg you now, for just a little while, to speak in English for the sake of our English friend by my side, who naturally does not speak Dansk.

'Since I love you all, I will come round to kiss some of you. We play Confessions! Those whom I kiss must then say if they are happy or not in this life and give reasons. Just a sentence or two and then you get another kiss, or a bite on the ear.'

The speech raised a lot of laughter and comment. I thought she staggered slightly as she started on her rounds. At Jannick's chair, she stopped and gave him a lingering kiss on the lips, to which he responded warmly, wrapping an arm round her shoulders.

'Oh, what a brother!' she gasped. 'Why have we never committed incest? Jannick, say if you are happy or not in this life.'

Jannick stood up rather drunkenly, laughing, to say, 'With such a sister like this one, who could be unhappy? Yes, my life's okay, Ingrid, sweetheart, and one day before I am too bald I will become manager of my company.'

'Then we can all be rich!' Ingrid shrieked. She was well into her performance now, calling as she went, amid sly remarks from the other guests, 'I love you so much, I sleep with you all and you all sleep with each other.'

The game went on, with Ingrid rushing round about the table, waving her arms excitedly. Most people declared their happiness at being present on this occasion. An elderly lady, having received Ingrid's kiss, said, 'My husband died since five years. Frankly, it was a relief. I don't wish for any sex, only pleasant male company. I have a little house on the Swedish archipelago, where I remain in the summer. There I sun myself and take it easy. I would say I am content.'

131

A pretty blonde young cousin, not more than twenty-five years old, was next for the kiss. Ingrid flung herself upon her, kissed her deeply, rubbed her breasts, while the girl squeaked. 'Oh, you are so gorgeous, Liss, I could easily have an affair with you! Once I was like you, long before men ruined me. You honey-pot, tell me you are happy with your life!'

The girl, looking considerably flustered, said, 'Please, Ingie, I can't tell if I'm happy. We are all so spoilt and so prosperous. What do we do with our lives? Are we just supposed to be like this, having parties and sex and drink and drugs and everything – in a world starving, and with many wars? I am so useless. I think it always.'

Ingrid's response was admirable in my eyes. She kissed the girl more gently, saying, 'You make us all happy by being here. Now, that is not useless!'

The kisses and confessions continued. Ingrid was getting drunker, snatching drinks from guests' glasses as she passed. Everyone was excited, urging her on, laughing, cheering.

When she reached my chair, we kissed deeply. She proclaimed in a scream, 'This is the man I love the most!' to great applause. She had already made such an announcement twice before to others.

'We cannot expect to be happy all the time. It is sufficient to be happy tonight, and to be in company with people like Jannick and Ingrid. I say – may tonight continue forever!'

As I sat down, she whispered, 'Meet me outside in ten minutes.'

Many people were on their feet now. Jannick took over his sister's role, and ran about kissing the girls, hardly waiting for them to make their statement. Under the pretence of looking for the toilet, I sneaked out of the back door. The chill of evening hit me. I was dizzy with drink. I peed into a bush.

In the front of the house, the cars were whales beached on the pavement. I tried several doors. Finding one that opened, I got in and sat there. With English instinct, I had chosen the left-hand door, and so found myself behind the steering wheel. By luck, I had picked Ingrid's car; in a minute, she came and sat in the front seat, throwing herself on me.

We kissed.

'Oh, Ingrid, what fun you are!'

'We must not be bored. The evening was getting boring.'

She was searching in her handbag for something. I saw a glint of keys in there, reached in, snatched the keys out. The one that was clearly the car ignition key I thrust into the ignition, starting the engine.

'What're you doing? Are you mad?'

I backed out of the narrow space and swung the car onto the road, to charge down it at a great pace in first gear.

'Stop, you fool, stop! What do you do? You can't drive in Denmark!'

'Left or right at the end? Quick! Quick! Which way?'

'No, no, we must stay at the party. It's right, turn right! They will miss us!'

'They're pissed.' I swung hard over to the right, flipping on the headlights as we ran onto a broader road. A man out walking his dog jumped for his life.

'You nearly killed him! Stop! Stop! You're mad!'

'He was in the bloody way. Now where?'

'You're on the wrong side of the road.'

'Bugger!' I swerved violently, to avoid an oncoming car by inches.

'Oh, Christ! Left here. Slow down, will you?'

Houses and lights swept away in a blur.

'Ingrid, apologies, but I've got to get you back to the fucking summerhouse. I must have it up you.'

'So you kidnap me! Slow down. Mind these people. Turn right here.'

We were on the back road. I managed to drive without going

133

into the ditch. I slowed. I stopped. I got out and went round the car to help her out. But she was out already. Slamming the door shut, we ran to their garden and into the summerhouse.

'No lights! The girls might see us.'

'I don't care. I must have it up you, I must! Shit!'

I was falling over, trying to get out of my trousers.

'What are you doing, for God's sake? Can't we talk? You're pissed!'

'Get your clothes off. I've longed for you all day. Come here.'

'But the party – '

'What do you think I came to Denmark for?' I was laughing, she giggling.

'Torskerogn,' she kept saying, in answer to my question. 'Torskerogn, of course.'

'Your fanny! Understand? I must kiss your fanny.' We were struggling in the dark, she fending me off feebly, as if it were a game.

'No, no, you can't. I must go back to the party.'

'I must kiss your gorgeous fanny first.'

Her panties were flimsy little things. I dragged them down her legs. She kicked them away, and was making a struggle of some kind, maybe to add to the excitement. Once I had my hand on her fanny, there was no more resistance. 'Oh, oh, sweetheart…' she murmured, incoherently.

We were perched on the edge of a sofa. Sliding off onto my knees, I managed to get my tongue between her lower lips. She was not particularly hairy. I hardly heard her groans, since I was making similar noises of delight myself, as she slid closer to the horizontal, parting her thighs to allow me deeper into that hot little grotto. How I loved its creamy contents, the taste, the feel, the experience, the conflagration at the centre of the glow-worm world! Then I began to rub the charmed spot. As she writhed, so she slipped down beside me.

'Grab my prick!'

She grabbed it and began kissing its stem, whilst keeping up a low-intensity squeak of desire. Could we see in the dark?

It was as if neither of us could let go of the prize we had at our fingertips. How can I describe that great ocean of feeling in which we were being carried? If you have swum in its depths, then you will understand; if you have never swum there… Well, what is my book doing in a monastery?

As for those murmured nothings, when set down on the page they do not carry with them the fragrant breezes of desire that once filled their sails.

'Oh, I love you so. I always did. I need you inside me. Stick this thing inside me.'

As rabbit into rabbit hole… Female flesh encloses you. Your entire sensibility pursues it.

'Oh, that delectable quim of yours… I always desired you! I'm in there! Right in!'

'Oh, I need it. Why fool about? More, more…'

She was practically on top of me. I munched on a breast like a mango. Then she plunged her lovely tongue deep into my mouth. All our salivas were functioning, and we were gasping at the same time, 'Oh, you're mine, you're mine. I've needed you…' And other such incoherencies. 'You can't know how I feel…' 'I feel the same…'

'Brilliant…'

'Beautiful…'

With our breathed words went that continued movement, rocking back and forth, little more than six inches in either direction, yet making irresistible progress towards fulfilment…

This is hardly the time for interruptions, but if you are worried about adultery, let me tell you that when you reach my age, all the women who are attractive come with blokes attached. The ones who are free are rejects from the pastures of sex. Once you draw your old age pension, adultery attains, if not legality, compulsory status. It's okay – you have only a few years to go.

Wave on wave of fruitful feeling, on and on, striving strongly, out into the most orchidaceous of oceans, lovely Ingrid and I, afloat together, blissful, naked bums going like fiddlers' elbows.

Then we were beached at last. 'Next time, from behind,' she whispered.

Chapter Seven

It is much to be regretted, not least by any serious critic, that I should have wasted time describing my insignificant pleasures in Denmark. However, they were far from insignificant to me. One thing that made me feel triumphant afterwards was that my little soldier had stood up for himself, and did not perform his usual cowardly act of retreating before a shot was fired. I could hardly imagine how it had happened. Perhaps it was because I had not been thinking about it.

Of course, while Ingrid and I were in the throes, much more important events were taking place in the great world where Archie Langstreet operated and the World Health Organisation did its good work for humanity.

Langstreet had gone back to Crete. He had resigned from the WHO, only three months before his retirement was due.

Now he was once more in Kyriotisa – a Kyriotisa which, said the mayor, was now 'on the map'. Langstreet sat listening to Mayor Paskateris in the mayor's little hot parlour looking on to Memorial Square. The mayor was a man in his forties, pleasant if rather ordinary-looking, clean-shaven, thin, and at present anxious to please.

Paskateris spent a while praising Langstreet's fortitude in

returning to the town. Langstreet had been badly treated on his previous visit to Crete, for which treatment he, as mayor, was deeply ashamed. Despite which, Langstreet and his family had shown great good will towards Crete and, indeed, to Kyriotisa itself; for which he, the mayor, and indeed the whole of Kyriotisa, and places beyond, were grateful.

In particular, Langstreet had drawn the world's attention to this poor, humble town, as a repository of works of art dating from the distant past. But it was by that generous gesture that difficulties were accumulating which were entirely beyond the resources of a poor town to resolve.

Visitors were flocking to Kyriotisa to view the chapel in which the original painting of Agia Anna hung. They consisted mainly of two kinds: visitors who were arriving out of curiosity, and the more religiously minded – pilgrims, in fact. Many visitors of both kinds were Americans. They were full of complaints. They could not acquire brochures or souvenirs. There was no good camera shop. There was no adequate accommodation. Also, the way to the little chapel was so long, and difficult to negotiate in high heels. The lane was narrow, winding, and choked with coaches. There were no comfort stations on the way.

As yet, the stream of visitors was but a tinkle (said the mayor). As it grew, so problems would increase intolerably. They had some illness problems, and ladies with twisted ankles. Yet the nearest hospital was in Hania. This was why he, Mayor Paskateris, was seeking advice from Langstreet. What should they do? How might the tourists be satisfied? More importantly – but it was the same question, he said, with a melancholy gesture – how could Kyriotisa benefit from this extraordinary turn of events?

While they discussed the matter, the mayor wished to reveal a further difficulty he was facing. Here he requested his secretary to leave the room, so that he might speak confidentially to his distinguished guest. Many visitors who had seen the shrine and the crude painting of Agia Anna, defaced by time, had expressed

138

disappointment. The ikon they had seen reproduced, which had lured them to this inaccessible region of Crete, had been so clear and pure. The actual painting seemed to them fraudulent.

In the wall-painting, the eyes of both Anna and the Holy Child had been scratched out. Why, tourists were asking, were the eyes not reinstalled and the painting repainted?

'You see, my dear sir, more funding is required. Iraklion will grant us no more funds. Between us, I may say, sir, that Iraklion is jealous of our success, since we draw the crowds from visiting the palace at Knossos.'

'Possibly I can be of some assistance. At least we might have the lane paved.'

'It would be a start.'

In a rear parlour, a light lunch was served. The two men drank mineral water with their taramasalata and feta salad.

Over coffee, Langstreet asked to see a map of the area. Paskateris went to phone a local architect, to whom he had lent his only map. When the architect turned up, he proved to be a bright young Athenian, by name Takis Constantinou, and the compiler of the map – of which he brought a photocopy to spread before them.

The mayor introduced Langstreet as Director of ACDW. Langstreet corrected him; he was now retired.

Constantinou traced, with a well-manicured finger, the route from Kyriotisa, off the main road, down the lane, to the olive grove where the Agia Anna chapel stood.

The mayor said, 'The coaches must stop on the road here. Then the visitors and pilgrims must walk down the lane for two kilometres, and into the field to the chapel. It's a bad arrangement.'

'Who owns the lane?' Langstreet asked.

'I do. It is in my family for generations. And the land around, including the olive groves.'

'Ah ha,' said the young architect. 'Then there is not a problem. We build a good coach park on the hill, by the main road, and no one has to walk down the lane at all.'

'How do they get to the chapel?' Langstreet asked.

The architect had not thought of that. 'By a monorail?'

The two older men looked at each other. They started to laugh. In the silence that followed, fingers drummed on tabletops.

Finally, Langstreet said, 'At least we could resolve one of the difficulties by building a coach station on the hill, by the main road. There can be toilet facilities – '

'A souvenir shop?' suggested the architect.

'Possibly, yes. What do you think, Paskateris?'

'There is an insuperable objection. I own the land – that's true – but a clause in the family deeds makes it impossible for me ever to build on the land. It has to be preserved intact, I regret.'

'I need to make some phone calls,' Langstreet said. 'Let's meet again tomorrow.'

Constantinou asked if he might be with them again. He had some good ideas.

When Langstreet walked to the mayor's offices next morning, he observed some of the changes to Kyriotisa. Two coaches had arrived from Hania. They were parked in the main square. Their drivers smoked contentedly in the sun. The tourists decanted from the coaches were not having the best of times. No taxis or cars were to be rented; such as there were had already left.

The tourists standing about unhappily were faced with a two-mile walk to the Agia Anna chapel. Or they could stay in Kyriotisa to savour its limited delights.

Carpenters working on two shops along the main drag were busy changing their facades. One of them already sported a sign: OPNING SOON: THE PARTHENON COFEE PARLOR. Tourists stood in the road nearby, as if waiting for the Parthenon to open.

Paskateris and Constantinou were already talking together over coffee when Langstreet entered the offices. Constantinou cordially offered Langstreet a Carter.

When the preliminaries were over, the mayor said, 'I can sell you the land at a reasonable price. Then you can build on it. The restriction is circumvented because you are a foreigner.'

'We can have something grand here. A new cinema would be best. I will draw up plans,' Constantinou announced.

Langstreet became very serious. He explained that he was now retired, after a busy public life. If he bought the land – even if he bought it very cheaply – he would be buying responsibility for which he was unprepared. He regretted that he was not prepared to get involved to such an extent.

The discussion continued for an hour, before the mayor had to leave on other business. He apologised for the interruption, but would be back later. Meanwhile, in a courteous manner, he thanked Langstreet again for returning to his, the mayor's, impoverished town, and for his noble concern in this matter of merely local importance.

He said that Constantinou would keep Langstreet company until he returned early in the afternoon. But Langstreet preferred his own company, considering the architect a silly man, and his idea of building a cinema a ridiculous proposition. He whiled away his time walking about the streets of Kyriotisa until they were all familiar to him and he knew personally at least half-a-dozen skulking hounds.

The sun was already lost behind the mountains when Mayor Paskateris returned, full of apologies for the delay.

'We can settle this matter between us,' he said. 'Preferably over a meal,' he added, 'for which the department will be honoured to pay.'

They went to a small restaurant where, after voluble consultation with the owner in his kitchen, they decided upon a *kghidtha*, a dish of goat's meat, served with tomato sauce and a salad. Paskateris ordered a bottle of retsina, with a glass of which he toasted Langstreet.

'Thanks to you,' he said, 'there is a chance that this poor town may get more securely on every map.'

They were some way through the meal when Takis Constantinou entered the restaurant. His expression was dark and sulky. He said in sarcastic tone, 'I did not receive your note that we were to meet again.'

'The mayor was late,' said Langstreet, with a hint of apology.

Paskateris was more effective. Waving Constantinou into a chair at the table, he said bluntly, 'I cannot persuade Mr Langstreet to enter into our future plans.'

'I can't become involved,' said Langstreet, still apologetic, 'as I have explained. Except to wish you well. I have business in England.'

Constantinou beckoned the manager to bring him a glass. When it came, with a nod at the mayor, he poured himself some retsina from the bottle.

A silence was broken by the architect. 'If it's a question of money – '

'It is not a question of money,' Langstreet said firmly. 'I would like to do what I can for Kyriotisa, which has so many sad memories, but I cannot undertake the responsibility...'

'If it was a question of money, what I was going to say was, if we built a cinema here you would probably get your investment back in under two years.' Constantinou leant forward to make this announcement, looking very shrewd at the same time, while pointing a finger ahead to indicate the direction of his idea. 'An open-air cinema.'

'No cinema,' said Langstreet. 'I must be firm. It is a holy ikon people come to see. They come in reverence. They want no distractions from cinemas. A small replica shrine, maybe, standing perhaps at the entrance to the coach station.'

After a tense silence, the mayor said, 'You cannot make any such reservations, Mr Langstreet, unless you are a partner in the use of the ground. You must appreciate that.'

Langstreet nodded. He went over to the window and gazed into the gathering dusk.

Last night, he had had an hour's phone discussion with his

financial advisors in London. They had recommended him not to make any investment in this poor part of the world.

Yet he felt a commitment. He was a wealthy man. He could change the way these people lived! Turning, he told the mayor that he must speak to his wife in Geneva. He dialled from a stifling restaurant kiosk. A message awaited him on the answerphone. Kathi had left for London.

He phoned their apartment in Harrington Gardens, Kensington.

When Kathi answered, he began to discuss with her the possibility of purchasing the land outside Kyriotisa, going into some detail about what could be done with it to make access to the Agia Anna shrine easier. She listened in silence for a while.

When, finally, Langstreet's exposition ceased, Kathi said:

'I have only two questions to ask. The first is this: why should you involve yourself further in the affairs of that dreadful part of the world, where we had so much trouble, where I nearly got shot? It has nothing to do with the case against Nentelstam. That's all over. You're retired. Why have anything more to do with Kyriotisa?'

He stumbled over his reply.

'I must do this, Kathi. There's a moral imperative. Kyriotisa was once prosperous. The war ruined it. Now a growing tourist trade gives it an opportunity to revive. I must help that process. I feel I owe it to them.'

'You owe them nothing. The decline of Kyriotisa's prosperity began long before the war. It's the family connection with the wartime invasion that worries you, isn't it?'

'Well, no, not really. I mean, we saw how desperate – '

'Archie, dear, you're trying to deceive yourself. You're still trying to prove there are good Germans. Even though you are not a German. You have a British passport. You do not have to ruin yourself to prove anything.'

She heard him groan. 'I'm still German at heart, Kathi. Are you not still a Romanian Jew at heart? Isn't that in part why I love you?'

Silence over the phone. She said in a cold voice, 'We are not discussing love at present.'

She believed she detected a slight quiver in his voice when he said that he did love her.

'We should not be speaking of these matters over the phone. They cut to the heart.'

She paused to control her voice. 'We should be sitting together so that we can hold each other's hands and look into each other's eyes for the truth. Can't you understand I have no guilt about being a Hungarian Jew? Whereas you still feel guilt about being – having been – having had a father who… Oh, shit… Give it up, Archie. Come back to Kensington and let's be reasonable and forget all about Crete.'

'I can't, my dearest. I must stay with what we have begun. After all, this was your idea – '

She rang off.

He sat by the phone, resting his brow in his hand. His forehead dripped sweat in the enclosed booth. He imagined his wife, sturdy in her dark dress. He saw her physical presence, which embodied her clever, logical mind, her independence, and her loyalty. His mind ran back and forth like a bear in a narrow cage.

After five minutes, he rang Kathi again.

'Yes?'

'You told me you had two questions to ask me. What was the second question?'

She was silent. Then she said, 'I am about to go out to a concert, Archie, and am already late.' Her detached tone reached him in his silent hotel room. 'I did not wish to ask this second question of you. That I had it in mind proves I had already guessed what your answer to my first question would be. My question is quite practical. What is the point of laying out money to construct this coach station and so on when people – flocks of people, it may be – will still have to walk down that lane we walked, two kilometres in the heat, only to find at the end of it

144

a pokey little chapel which will not hold more than half a dozen people at a time?'

'Well, I suppose they'll have to form a queue. Pilgrims are used to waiting.'

'And suppose it rains?'

'We could supply umbrellas.'

'And the ground turns to mud? Clogs? And the lane to a river? Boats?'

'We could provide shelters.'

'Nonsense, Archie! How long are people going to put up with that, with standing in an olive grove, waiting to get into that rotten little cattle shed? The trade will die as soon as it begins.

'For God's sake, if you must go into this, then think financially. Your investment – our money – will be lost. You'll just have ruined the countryside. Do think about these things. Come back to London and think about these things. Now I must dash away! I'm halfway to the door!'

Langstreet left the booth, mopping his face. He returned to the meal table, where his dish, for which he had little appetite, was growing cold.

He addressed the mayor and the architect. 'I am prepared to invest in such tourist amenities as will contribute to Kyriotisa's finances. That is to say, if you will meet my conditions.'

The mayor mumbled something encouraging and accepted one of Constantinou's cigarettes.

'What is needed is an overall plan, not just piecemeal thinking. There is a way in which we can facilitate conditions for tourists – for pilgrims – which will be profitable for us investors and the neighbourhood.'

When Archie had outlined his plan, Mayor Paskateris rose to his feet.

'It is a brilliant plan. I see everything in my eye's mind. We shall follow it to the letter.'

He held out his hand.

145

While these great affairs were coming to fruition, affairs on which the prosperity of a region and perhaps the faith of the religious depended, I was still having to live out my life in the un-narrated hinterlands of my novel.

My love affair with Ingrid caused me some guilt, as well as some apprehension; for if Sven found out about us, he would probably have attacked Ingrid. What else do you expect? I moved to a room in a small hotel in Kastrup. Ingrid visited me there, and we talked about poetry and the fate of the world.

Ingrid told me the reason for her hatred of her husband. She had a friend, Loretta Bouillard, a French woman who had worked in the French film industry. Loretta had come to her one day with some pictures she had downloaded from her computer. The pictures had been circulating on the Web. They showed three girls cavorting naked on a beach.

In some pictures, the girls were performing cartwheels, thus exposing their delicate genitalia. In other pictures they were rather lewdly showing off these underdeveloped parts of their pubescent and pre-pubescent bodies to the camera.

Ingrid recognised the girls as her daughters, Lisa, Dorothea, and Sigbrit. Sven had made money from their daughters' nudity. She burned with shame.

She could work out when the photographs had been taken. Through the contact with Loretta, Ingrid occasionally acted as an extra in a film. The job provided her with pocket money, supplementing her salary at the university. One such film had been shot in the spring. Ingrid had gone up to Jutland to play her modest part. She had left the girls in Sven's care.

On her return home, she had found Lisa silent and downcast. The trip to Paleohora had been an attempt to cheer up her elder daughter. The girls had sworn that their father had not molested them in any way. There had been only that one day on the beach, when he had forced them to do what Dorothea called 'naughty poses'. Lisa, the oldest girl, had been deeply shamed when forced to exhibit herself.

At the time, Ingrid, in a fury, had broken into Sven's desk and found a collection of child pornography. She had thrown the photographs and magazines all round the room and had a furious row with Sven. However, since he swore he had not molested the girls, but merely, in his words, 'photographed them at their prettiest', Ingrid had continued to live with him: for financial security, she claimed. Yet she admitted that the knowledge they held between them had made them more sexually active.

I too became transfixed by these passions. Nor could I remain with the daughters without seeing them in my mind's eye on the beach, legs spread, inviting they knew not what with their bright, fixed expressions. Lisa was Lucia's age when Lucia and I had met. Far less sophisticated.

Under her cheerful demeanour, Ingrid was a troubled person. She had some friends who met for group sex sessions once a week. They had drinks and vegetarian snacks before removing their clothes. Ingrid wished us to join them.

'Ingrid, I can't. I'm old. I have but one shot in my locker per day, if that. Your friends will not want an old man with grey hair in their midst.'

'Come and watch the rest of us going at it. Sometimes we have daisy chains. That would inspire you.'

'Maybe, but no thanks.'

'Oh, you are such a prude.'

'Unfortunately, I am an old prude…'

However, I did go with her to see her act as an extra in another film being shot at Helsingor, where Hamlet's castle stood. Ingrid was needed only for a crowd scene; it was a day's work, no more. The movie was entitled, *Gertrude's Golden Days*. The company filming it was American.

I stood with a roped-off section of spectators to watch the proceedings. After an hour of waiting, the cameras began to turn and the star of the movie appeared on the castle battlements.

I recognised her. It was Sylvia Beltrau, as she now was, the

147

transformed Lucia: painted, made blonde, jewel-bedecked and padded, eyes loaded with kohl and mouth with lipstick, with all her genuine character and characteristics blotted out, until only an avenging, commercialised shell remained.

It was time to return to England.

The months cantered through their loops like demented cantaloupes. I maintained a low profile. I rented a couple of rooms in Ossington Street, consorting fairly often with my literary agent and friend, Will Welling-Jones, the chap who had a big wife, mentioned earlier. We would meet at my club, the Groucho, for a glass of wine, and then stroll up the street to the Red Fort for a buffet lunch with some friends. The food was good and delicately flavoured. One served oneself from huge copper drums.

A frequent topic of conversation was my novel, *New Investments*. It had not sold very well in hardcover, but Will's media agent worked in liaison with a media agent in Hollywood, who had sold a nine month option on the novel to an outfit working closely with Columbus Films. A beggarly sum was involved, good for a few lunches at the Red Fort, but better things were promised if Columbus Films bought the proposal. We lived in hope.

No denying that it was a pretty miserable period as far as I was concerned. Sylvia Beltrau's lawsuit still threatened, although its force had diminished considerably since her movie, *Something to Behold*, had failed rather noticeably at that box which, as effectively as another box, the coffin, seals our fate: the box office. The one slice of luck I had was in finding a bootleg video in Cecil Court, entitled *Carole Lombard Strips Off*. She certainly does, to good effect, if in black and white.

Meanwhile, I was doing some reviewing for a small literary magazine, the editor of which I had met at university. The work did not pay, but one could sell the books afterwards. Most people regard reviewing as an excuse to make a few clever remarks at the author's expense – like the chap who said, regarding one of my early novels, *The Banners of Barabas*, 'Not only does he write spuriously of the past, but he awakens in the reader a spurious desire for a spurious past'.

You see, I still remember it word for word. But the fact is, after reading that criticism, I never again attempted another historical novel. How can we get right the details and detailed feelings of the world before our own and our parents' lifetimes? It's almost as bad as setting a novel a hundred years in the future. From the time I read those unkind words in print, I have always stuck to stories set in the present day (fortunately no one knows what actually goes on in the present); so perhaps cruelty has its benefits.

The funny thing is, that historical novel is still in print in paperback, thirty years after first publication. Two years ago, it was a set book for GCSE.

Some evenings, I simply sat in my room, watching soaps on the box. Viv Baker was still working in her West End clothes shop. The part was no longer being played by Doreen Stephens, alias Diana Coventry. Dear old Doreen. I still missed her. What do you expect?

As well as the reviewing, I continued work on this novel. I rather wondered if I might improve the tone of it by bringing in some resemblances between Archie Langstreet and Oedipus. Oedipus kills his father and marries his mother unknowingly. It makes no difference that he does these things in ignorance. He must be punished for them. Langstreet is committing a serious crime with the best of intentions. Should I draw a parallel between the two men?

No, I thought. Too pretentious by half. Too forced. Was the mere idea a sign that I was running out of material?

As to that, while I was living my idle and useless life, great things were happening in Crete. Langstreet had removed Takis Constantinou from the scene and engaged a Japanese architect and a Taiwanese construction team to build what Kathi called, with some disdain, The Agia Anna Theme Park. Work had gone ahead at a steady pace.

The coach station outside Kyriotisa also boasted a helicopter pad; well-heeled pilgrims could fly in from Hania or even Piraeus, without having to endure the tiring coach trip over the mountains. In the station itself, a cafeteria and restaurant greeted them, with limited accommodation above (an on-site hotel was at the planning stage).

Best of all, however, was a large-scale replica of the chapel down the hill. This chapel, The Chapel of Agia Anna, was provided with a proper door through which one could enter without stooping. The interior was well lit. The walls were decorated with frescos in the Byzantine manner, chief among which was an imitation of Monaché Kostas' fake ikon of the Suckling Event (as the guide book has it).

Assistants saw to it that there was a regular throughput in the chapel, their authority reinforced by a sign saying: NO PRAYING IN THIS CHAPEL. One left by a rear door equipped with turnstile. Conveniently placed outside were toilets and a bookshop, which sold postcards, videos, CDs, DVDs, guide books, and of course replicas of the Anna ikon and other sacred ikons. In one corner of the shop sat Monaché Kostas himself. There he sat, in new robes, painting, fulfilling the need for local colour. He had been lured from his gorge by a small monthly payment.

I had been reviewing a new illustrated edition of Trollope's *Autobiography*. I was struck by the passage where Trollope says, 'When I sit down to write a novel I do not at all know, and I do not very much care, how it is to end'. He contrasts this devil-may-care attitude with Wilkie Collins' method of careful planning. I believe it was this remark of Trollope's that drove him out of favour for many years. It caused him not to be regarded as a Serious Artist.

It was hard at that moment not to wish that my practice was less like Trollope's in this respect: I was not sure what should come next. Like Trollope, I was making it up as I went along (this was the only resemblance between us, by the way). But serendipity came to my aid. Serendipity is always on a writer's side. Serendipity is always on a writer's side. (I repeat the remark in case it did not register the first time.)

I was enjoying a constitutional in Kensington, having taken a look at Kensington Gardens. A taxi drew up to the pavement in front of me. From it stepped an attractive lady, smartly dressed, with a floral hat such as ladies wear at weddings and, so I believe, Ascot. Accompanying her was an old man in a morning coat, clutching a grey topper. As she turned to give the old boy a hand, I recognised her. It was Kathi Langstreet.

She was surprised to see me – as well she might be, considering that we inhabited two different universes. As usual she was pleasant and polite with none of the frostiness the English mistake for politeness. Having paid off the taxi, she introduced the old man she was accompanying as her kind Uncle Antal. She introduced me by saying, 'He's writing about me.' Uncle Antal tried to look gladdened by the news, gazing up at me with the eyes of a myopic mackerel. As he and I shook hands, Kathi invited me into their hotel.

They were staying in the Claireville Gardens Hotel, a comfortable establishment with a large lounge, in which settles invited one to take one's ease. At one end was a generous bar, where some men were sitting on leather stools, talking and laughing. It was all pleasantly and unostentatiously English. A slender young woman was dancing naked to the sound of a grand piano, rattling bracelets on her pale arms.

A waiter appeared promptly, and Kathi ordered tea and sandwiches for the three of us.

She said that she and her uncle had been attending the marriage of Clifford, her stepson, to a lady called Vibe.

'It was lovely,' she said. 'So much more fun than weddings used to be. Less formal, y'know? Three young men, friends of the bride,

151

came forward as a trio, and sang a love song, 'I'm Old-Fashioned', which charmed everyone. It was all good and affectionate, wasn't it, Uncle?'

But Uncle Antal had drifted off to sleep, his worn old head resting on a cushion.

'He's in a dream,' she said, whirling a finger just above head level to indicate as much by signs. I saw that she was slightly tipsy.

'I danced after the ceremony,' she said. 'I even did the Twist! At my age!'

'Archie's not with you?' I ventured, after some polite exchanges had passed between us.

She made a moue of displeasure. 'Oh, he considered he was duty-bound to go and sort out a problem with the new hotel in Kyriotisa... This hotel of his is entirely new, sited beside the church and churchyard.'

'A second hotel?'

'It's part of a new scheme. The first hotel on the coach park is quite modest. There is considerable demand from tourists for a more luxurious hotel – five-star and all that – in the town. The foundations are already laid. Now a new problem has sprung up, a question of ownership of the actual land.'

'For this reason he fails to attend his son's wedding?'

She gazed down at her hands, without replying. When I repeated my question, she said, without looking up, 'You can see he's not here, can't you?'

We drank tea in silence. I noticed an odd detail about this very English scene. On the walls were hung, not the sporting or hunting prints one might have expected – presumably all of those had been exported to ritzy American hotels – but framed reproductions of the flamboyant portraits of Tamara de Lempicka. I wondered if you would classify de Lempicka as post-art-deco, or perhaps she was the one and only female vorticist?

I asked Kathi, 'Would you say that Tamara de Lempicka was the one and only female vorticist?'

She rolled her eyes. 'Oh, hell,' she said.

Perhaps feeling she had been too hard on her husband, she said, 'Archie's dedicated himself to the ambitious idea of restoring the fortunes of the area around Kyriotisa... He's investing very heavily.'

'Do you go to see how the work is progressing?'

Kathi cast a half-smile in my general direction. 'I hear enough about it over the phone. There was a feature in the *Daily Telegraph* on Monday. In any case, I imagine the whole place is covered with flying dust...'

I chewed one of the pale little sandwiches while I thought about it. Then I said, between mouthfuls, 'Kathi, forgive my saying so, but in my judgement your husband is making a monumental mistake. Isn't self-aggrandisement really his motive, nothing more than that? Why should he care about this dump, Kyriotisa? Why should he waste his and your money on such an enterprise? Isn't it just to make him feel like a big man in a small world?'

Her face, when she turned it to me, was luminous with anger.

She spoke calmly, in terms of contempt. 'Who are you to criticise? Archie is at least trying to do good, from whatever motive. When did you ever try to do good, you and your lascivious little affairs? You're all for yourself, aren't you?'

'It's a jungle out there, Kathi. What do you expect?'

'What do I expect?! Look, if you were a real writer, then you would write against the system. Isn't that a writer's first duty? Not just to make a piffling bit of money – to speak out and attempt to make the world a better place? At least Archie tries to do that!'

There was some truth in her words. I felt it bitterly. 'Do you believe the world can be improved?' I asked, by way of defence. 'I rather like the old dump as it is.'

'You are so negative!'

It was my turn to make no response. I ate another delicate sandwich.

When she made a move to waken her uncle, declaring that she would take him up to his bed where he could sleep more comfortably, I put out a detaining hand, saying gently that the old man was perfectly happy, asleep where he was, and that I would like to take this opportunity to ask her more about herself, if she would permit it.

To which, with a shake of her head, she claimed she had already told me all about herself. I argued that she had told me about things which had happened to her, but nothing of her inner self.

'My inner self? Suppose I don't have an inner self? I could tell you I was born in December of such-and-such a year, but what would it mean? I am also millions of years old – or all the components of my body are – recycled through eons of space and time. Does that satisfy you? As for what you might call my inner processes, most of them have come down to me on a living stream, from generation to generation, merging, blending, struggling to make sense of contradictory inheritances… "Little enough" is what I could label me. And that is probably the least interesting part…'

'Kathi, I'm sorry you're feeling so bad!'

She spread her hands. 'Forget it. It's probably the champagne speaking. Anyhow, I don't want your compassion.'

She roused her old uncle, who allowed himself, protesting feebly, to be led towards the elevators. As they went, Kathi said over her shoulder, 'Finish the sandwiches. You look as if you're down on your luck.'

There was something in what Kathi said. Although I must say in my own defence that being down on one's luck is fairly normal for writers. That is, real writers who write only novels and short stories and do not appear on chat shows or TV quizzes, or generally hold forth as if they know it all. It isn't everyone who can improve the world.

At the time I met Kathi, I was seeing not only my doctor but, even worse, my publisher. The doctor gave me some pills for my legs and a consoling word about my virility. To wit, 'Don't worry about it. Many men of your age can't get it up any more.'

154

It was not a good time. One should be in high spirits when meeting one's publisher. Kathi's criticism of me had hurt. No matter what she thought of me, there was my writing to plead my case. I couldn't help thinking of Samuel Johnson's words to the Earl of Chesterfield: 'No man is well pleased to have his all neglected, be it ever so little'. *Be it ever so little...* Johnson must have had me in mind when holding forth.

Wilberforce Large's offices were situated in an inconvenient part of London, on the third floor of a big thirties office block. There lived my editor, Sam Bell, in a small office with a formidable number of typescript bundles near at hand. I liked Sam. Sam had attended my old college in Oxford, although ten years after I had left under what my friends described as 'a cloud'. Indeed, in happier days, I had often taken Sam for a drink, instead of sponging off him, the way authors usually do to their publishers.

I took the Northern Line tube to East Finchley, a long wearisome journey. I read *The Victor Hugo Club* on the way. And I wished I had had my hair cut, so as to look less run down. Once at East Finchley, I had to walk to Muswell Hill Broadway, since there seemed to be no buses running. Rain began to fall. A bit like King Lear, I had no coat or umbrella offering me protection.

As the rain came on determinedly, I thought perhaps I would afford a taxi; but the few taxis that passed were all taken. After all, what do you expect? I bought a tabloid newspaper at a newsagent to protect my head.

I was wet and miserable by the time I got to the Broadway.

A curious thing happened as I entered the rather dark lobby of the Wilberforce Large building, with its damp and muddy floor. There in one corner, by the lifts, was the very same naked dancer I had seen in the Claireville Gardens Hotel. Not a thing on, except for the bracelets which she still wore. She waggled her hips and shook the bracelets above her head in a most enticing way.

I had scarcely had the chance for a good look when the lift

155

descended, some fool burst out with a parcel under his arm, and the girl was gone.

Mystified, I went up to see Sam, damp and downcast.

Of course I was aware that I had missed the date on which my contract said I should have completed and delivered the novel. But writers were always doing that. Publishers rarely noticed or cared; they always had too many books on hand, and were perhaps relieved if one or more dropped out. But as a punctilious writer of the old school, I always tried to be on time. To maintain Sam's goodwill, I had got my agent to send him the first hundred pages of the novel, as a promise, a *bonne bouche*, a testament to my lasting ability to crop regularly.

Sam met me at the lift on the third floor and shook my hand. 'You're bit damp, old boy. No taxis?'

'Sam, who was that naked girl dancing in your foyer?' I asked. 'She wasn't a writer, was she?' I thought some pop singer might have been selling Sam her confessions.

He regarded me blankly. 'Are you joking? Come into my office, will you? Would you like a coffee?'

'It wasn't a ghost, was it?'

'Of course not.' I saw by the look on his face that he thought I had been drinking. The best idea seemed to be to drop the subject.

I settled in one of his very low modern chairs, to mop my neck with my handkerchief. I would solve the problem of getting out of it later. We chatted for a bit, mainly about *Sometimes I Won*, the memoirs of, and the repellent personality behind, a well-known politician. I had known this political person vaguely up at Oxford, and contributed an anecdote about how he had been smoking a ciggie – as we all did in those far off days – and had set light to his clothes in a drunken bout.

Sam took up a typescript I recognised as mine and wagged it at me. 'You have here a very strong theme, about Langstreet and his endeavours to promote a religious cult in – where is it? Greece?'

'Crete.'

'Crete. Right. Obviously. But I'm bound to say… Well, you do rather pad out the story with your own adventures. Amatory adventures. It's a bit boastful, I find, if not irrelevant. For instance, on page – '

'Hang on, how do you mean, boastful? I am quite frank about being a rather unsuccessful ladies' man. I am in my seventies, you know, and often feel it. What do you expect?'

'All these encounters with women. It's obvious they are made up.'

'Not at all. The world is full of mature women looking for a flutter.'

'Mm. Foreign women, would you say?'

He was silent for a moment, listlessly turning over the pages. 'I do slightly worry about the inconsistencies. At one point you say you are impotent. Yet you seem to manage well enough with – who is it? – yes, Ingrid, the Swedish bit.'

'Someone else on the flutter.' I wasn't going to tell him what hell it was never knowing on which occasions you would be able or not to get an erection. Research had shown it worked a bit better with a new woman. *And* there was Viagra, the blessed new panacea for the old and randy. I had in fact talked over this painful matter with Ingrid; but I wasn't going to go into the problem in depth with my editor. (Incidentally, I don't think I met any woman who was put out by my condition; most of them had met limp male organs before, it turned out. My appearance forewarned them against disappointment; they could see I was pretty ancient. In any case, it's always nice to be in bed with an amusing member of the opposite sex.)

'She wasn't Swedish. It was her husband who was Swedish. Sven.'

After a pause, he said, 'Then there's this other business.'

'The teat?'

'Not the teat. The cunnilingus. Some readers will be disgusted. You're always going down on women.'

157

'I've done some research into cunnilingus, Sam. In the British Library, I mean, as well as on the hoof.' I tried to explain how, when it came to *soixante-neuf* situations, by far the majority of instances in nineteenth and early twentieth-century porn were exclusively about fellatio. That was the case in both written and pictorial porn. Women had to do it to men but men rarely reciprocated. It was considered unclean.

'It's come into its own of recent decades,' I said. 'Enormous progress in standards of hygiene has been made, even in the years since the last world war. Personally, of course, but also in the laundering of clothes. An immense variety of cosmetics, perfumes and deodorants, have come on the market. All of which have made our intimate parts less welcome homes for bacterial hordes. It has become a pleasure – a connoisseur's pleasure – to go down on a woman.

'And of course there is the one undeniable human improvement made in the murky waters of the twentieth century. I mean, the improvement in the status of women. Women are seen at last as man's equals, not his servants or inferiors. His equals in desire. Cunnilingus is to be celebrated. Lesbians will tell you. Its popularity is a mark of the better times in which we live.'

'Foreign women, would you say?'

His question made me feel he was not attending.

'I might also add that most women anywhere adore it. It's pleasant for both parties – as an aperitif, if not as the main course.'

'Why don't you go and live on the Continent?' Sam asked.

The question silenced me for a moment, much as a clout round the ear will silence an obstreperous child. Perhaps my enthusiasm had run away with me. I could not determine whether or not there was an unpleasant racist twist to Sam's question.

'Well, isn't that another way in which life – at least in England – has improved?' I said, trying to keep a whine from my voice. 'We're not as xenophobic as formerly, are we? Foreign is as foreign does. Perhaps we owe much of our loss of sexual inhibition to what you might call "foreigners". As our eating habits have become more varied and exotic and enjoyable, so have our sexual habits.'

Sam sighed and took a gulp from his coffee cup. Then he spoke impatiently.

'You may argue that. But it's going to upset a lot of readers. It's just pornography. It's not everyone who finds this habit of yours enjoyable. Good old straight intercourse is certainly good enough for me.'

'Ah yes, "If it was good enough for my father, then it's good enough for me", eh, Sam? No – muff-diving, as our American friends tend to call it, has long been a sophisticated pleasure. How it thrills your partner! And the joy of having those trembling white thighs embrace your cheeks! Why, there's – '

Sam was half-heaving himself from his chair. 'Steady, old boy, that's enough. I've heard enough. Your jacket's steaming! You'll catch fire!'

I subsided. 'Catch cold, more like. It's such hell getting here.'

'Well, simply hire a cab… No problem… You hire a cab.' He spoke in a soothing voice, as to a juvenile, bound to irritate, spacing his words – you pause hire pause a pause *cab*.

'All I'm saying is that muff-diving is one more colour on the palette and palate of love. One has to add that not all snatches invite visual or glossal enjoyment. They vary in looks and tastes.' I was vexed with myself for using the term 'snatch'; it was not a word I usually employed. I sighed heavily. 'Also, the face is important. A beautiful face implies… Well, you imagine there's a – well, a correlation…'

Sam was becoming more gloomy as I spoke. He adjusted his tie, using the action as an excuse for shaking his head.

'I mean, if you take Hedy Lamarr…' But I dared not blunder on to the end of the sentence. It struck me, perhaps belatedly, that neither of us was greatly enjoying the conversation.

I became afraid he might bring up the absurd paedophile charge next.

Sam now looked as if professionally involved in a Gloom Promotion Campaign. He squared up my pages by holding them upright and banging the lower edges against his desk top; after which, he laid them aside with a moue of distaste.

'I suppose this teat-sucking is all part of this sucking obsession of yours,' he said – I thought in a rubbishy way.

Trying to make light of it, I replied that muff-diving was less an obsession than a question of taste; or a matter of last resort. However old and incapable one grew, one still had a tongue in one's head.

Apparently he had not heard. 'All right. I take your argument, but it's not a good idea to air your obsessions in public.'

'You mean like Joyce did? And Hemingway? And Kafka? And – '

'I mean that, in your case, I don't think it works at all well.'

We sat looking at each other, like picnickers staring out from under umbrellas at heavy rain. Perhaps he feared that I might feel he was a dull fellow when it came to sex – as indeed I did. Jerking suddenly into an assumed gaiety, he said, 'Heard a good joke going the rounds the other day – kind of thing you might enjoy. About how you should seduce a member of the opposite sex. If you're a man, you've got to be sincere, worship the dear creature, buy her clothes, send her flowers and a naughty novel – not too naughty! – take her to expensive restaurants, and so forth. Then she may yield. Whereas...' He paused, his heavy face imitating a smile. 'Whereas, if you're a woman, all you have to do is turn up naked with a bottle of Scotch under your arm.'

'Ha ha,' I roared. I had used that joke myself, several years before, in *The Banners of Barabas*. It had not been very funny then, but I had had the good taste to use vodka.

Solemnity was quickly restored. Sam laid a hand, as if in paternal blessing, on my pages of typescript. 'But we are going to have to pass on this one, old boy... Sorry. I have discussed it with my co-editor. Try something else for a change. We are currently planning a new series of guide books. *The Large Little Guides.* You wouldn't like to do one on Crete, would you?'

'Instead?'

He nodded. 'Instead.'

Vasari's doomy words about the painter Perugino came to mind: 'With the terror of poverty constantly preying on his mind, he undertook, in order to earn money, such work as he would probably not have looked at, had he had the means to live.'

Saying I would think about it, I returned to the outside world and the persistent rain. The tabloid collapsed soggily about my head.

Archie Langstreet had finished his frugal breakfast. He hunched himself over a serious article in a serious paper, headed 'THE AGONY OF SAINT ANNA'. The claim of the article was that the great majority of those who'd visited the shrine in the previous year had been women. When interviewed, many women saw Anna as an image of neglected motherhood; this was Anna's compelling power – an older woman maintaining her family over two generations without acknowledgement. 'She is a symbol of women's strength in sustaining the human race,' claimed a woman from Chicago, Ill. 'She's the lady who saved Jesus for the benefit of the human race,' claimed a lady from Paris, France. 'I love her more than the Blessed Virgin Mary,' said a teenager from Neustadt, Germany.

'Despite indications that the entire Agia Anna project is going pear-shaped – costing Archibald Langstreet most of his many millions,' concluded the article, 'it obviously affords consolation to millions of women.'

Perhaps it afforded some consolation to Langstreet as well.

He sat in his suite at his table, resting his chin in his hand and staring out of the window. A cup of coffee cooled by his elbow. He was, at this early hour, in his shirtsleeves.

Beyond the window, a man was working on a wooden platform,

applying rendering to the facade of the still unfinished hotel. He was now working at the second floor, where Langstreet had his suite of rooms, the ground and first floors being as yet incomplete.

The workman was of middle age. His clothes appeared at least as old as he. The lower part of his lined face was concealed by a beard and moustache. The hair of his head sprouted from beneath his cap like a small shelf, shielding his eyebrows. His tightly-closed lips held a dead cigarette end firmly in position. The business of rendering covered him with white, so that he looked ancient enough to have emerged from a recent ice age.

He worked steadily, occasionally pausing to remove the dead cigarette from his mouth and spit.

Langstreet felt contempt as well as admiration for this man. Contempt because (as far as he knew) this man had never tried to better himself, being resigned to remaining a labourer; admiration because the man worked so doggedly, almost without pause.

Whatever virtues the labourer possessed, his intellect had been stunted, his perspectives narrowed, by poverty. It was against such injustices that Langstreet imagined himself to be working – and on behalf of this ordinary man.

He had studied the man so long that he almost convinced himself he had seen him before; had he perhaps been one of the gang holding Cliff to ransom, and now at last in gainful employment?

Even as this notion crossed his mind, Langstreet dismissed it as a foolish fancy, drained his coffee cup, and rose to get on with his business of the morning.

The elevator was austere; dull metal doors flanked by metal panels. He admired it. The cage rose silently from its repose. The doors opened. He entered. When he pressed a button, the cage began its descent. Through the small window and the elevator entrance, where doors had yet to be installed, he saw the thrilling barrens of the first floor, as yet undecorated except by entanglements of cable hanging from the ceiling or snaking across the floor. Men were at work, glimpsed in frozen attitudes as the cage passed on down to the ground floor.

Here, Langstreet, ignoring groups of chattering tourists, went to the rear of the building. He entered the office, where secretaries were already at work. He greeted them absently. It was his hotel. He kept himself remote. Marigolds in a jug had been set on his desk. He moved them away, to a side shelf. The Formica shelves above, below, reflected their gold – but he had turned away.

His secretary had already opened up the computer. He scanned the emails. There was an explanation and an apology for delay from the Swiss company which made the elevators. The doors for the first and third floors would be delivered within ten days. A British firm acknowledged the acceptance of their estimate for bulletproof glass. Kathi sent a message saying, 'Hello, are you okay? Would love to hear from you.' He set it aside, sighing.

It was necessary to respond to the Historical Monuments department in Bonn. The department complained that the German war memorial, honouring the dead of both Greece and Germany, was being broken up. Langstreet replied that cruelty needed no monument. Torture, he wrote, was still in use by sixty different regimes over the globe. No one greatly minded. No one greatly minded the misery of poverty. He minded. The monument had served its purpose. The site was required for further development, and for the improvement of local living standards.

Next, Langstreet saw various dignitaries and property owners who voiced complaints of one kind or another. The most vocal was a man who lived by the church. He was suffering from the 'curse of foreign backpackers and New Age hippies', as he called them, who had filled the empty space behind his garden with their tawdry encampments. One young ruffian had actually climbed the fence and relieved himself in the complainant's garden. The music and noise of the backpackers was a constant source of misery; so much so that his wife was on the point of a breakdown.

Langstreet was calm and professional. He expressed sympathy, hoping for better times, explaining that all these troubles were merely the growing pains of Kyriotisa's return to its ancient prosperity.

He instructed his secretary on various items and then turned to the phone. After an hour of calls, he switched the phone off and went outside, into the dusty sunlight.

Looking up, he saw the renderer suspended high above on his platform, still spraying rendering on the concrete façade of the building.

Kyriotisa was wakening to a new place in the world. Despite the newly functioning coach station further down the road, coaches choked the street, many of them drawn up on the pavement, outside bars and an old hotel – practically a doss house, in Langstreet's opinion. In the dull, grey thoroughfare, the coaches bulged with colour – violet, purple, light blue, dark blue, crimson. Most of them bore German or Austrian registration plates.

It had already been decided by the local council that a road bypassing the main street of Kyriotisa should be built. EU money had been sought for this project. Distant roars indicated that work had already begun: the initial business of filling in an entire valley, obliterating what was green under what was a tumbled grey, with rubble and hardcore, to make a level foundation for the new road. Six dump trucks, fat as dung beetles, freshly shipped from Piraeus, laboured on the job in clouds of dull yellow dust. Gears ground, whistles blew, as the great task was co-ordinated.

A man came up and greeted Langstreet. He was the newly appointed chief of police for Kyriotisa, now that it had acquired fresh importance. At his invitation, Langstreet stepped into his open-top vehicle and they drove no more than a hundred and fifty metres to the site of the German war memorial.

Here was more activity. The sprawling monument was being broken up, on the grounds that its reminder of the past was no longer necessary; as the more distant past, represented by Agia

Anna, came into popularity, so the more recent past was rendered unnecessary, obtrusive. Besides, the memorial upset the new breed of German and Austrian tourists. There had been complaints. In place of this unfashionable and depressing object – occupying a 'prime site' – another hotel would grow, The Concord Hotel.

A line of young trees was being planted. They had been prematurely delivered, so they had to be dug in promptly; but the construction machinery would make short work of them. Standing to one side, slightly away from the cranes, bulldozers and lorries, a group of protesters stood with their placards. 'WHAT IS PASSED SHOULD NOT BE WIPED AWAY', said one placard. The protesters fell silent when they saw the police chief draw up.

'Let them protest,' he said as an aside to Langstreet. 'They do no harm.'

'They have a point.'

'We don't need that point. We need prosperity.' As they prowled round the front of the site, he said, 'You have no regret that your father's name is swept away?'

'None.'

There was so much marble dust in the air that they did not stay.

It was an ordinary scene of destruction. Neither Langstreet nor the police chief felt any strain as they went about what had already become their usual business. But behind the mundane, the extraordinary was raging to escape.

Chapter Eight

In such ways as these, Langstreet's days were passed. He had no more time to focus his attention on matters other than those involving the adoration of the Agia Anna ikon, than had the workman beyond his hotel window the ability to reflect on anything except his daily labour.

In March of that year, 1,245 foreign visitors came to Kyriotisa to see the ikon, exhibited in state in its new chapel. In April, the figure rose to 3,200. And in May the figure was 7,735, straining Kyriotisa's facilities and Hania's capacities to the limit. This last figure included many Greeks, who came from as far afield as Thessaloniki to see the ikon of Agia Anna.

Relating these events, I attempt a degree of realism. I realise this means the detailing of matters some might find sordid, but I swear by the self-exhortation Degas wrote in his notebooks: 'Do every kind of worn objects... Corsets which have just been taken off... Series on journeyman bakers, seen in the cellar itself or through the air vents from the street...' Such is the nature of the empirical investigation of human reality, no great and noble thing.

So it was that in May, Langstreet, returning to his hotel one Tuesday at noon, found an ambulance and a mob blocking the entrance. He pushed his way through and in an authoritative manner demanded to know what was happening. It was clear enough (though that did not stop a sycophantic youth explaining everything to the great man). The workman employed on rendering the hotel façade – the workman whom Langstreet had studied with interest – had fallen with his platform and was lying dead on the pavement below. His broken body was being stowed away in the ambulance. As well as the shattered wooden platform, chunks of the concrete façade lay about the blooded ground.

'Careless fools!' exclaimed Langstreet, pushing his way into the hotel, where he had a small bottle of gaseous mineral water, tara-masalata and toast, and a cup of coffee for lunch.

An email was delivered to his table. Kathi said she had not heard from him for some while. She worried about his health. She was going to fly over and see how he was. He pushed the note irritably to one side.

While he went about his ordinary business, the police held an enquiry into the cause of the death of the renderer. The construction company were charged with carelessness and negligence with regard to safety precautions. This was denied; the company claimed that the mobile platform from which the man worked was in no way at fault. The concrete facing on the crest of the hotel had crumbled and, in falling, had struck the platform, sending it and the worker crashing to the ground.

The construction company withdrew its labour until the matter was settled and the charge against them was dropped. They demanded compensation. The Japanese architect and two materials chemists arrived from Tokyo to defend the formula used for their concrete. They had won the contract only because their methods were believed (by the Greeks) to be more efficient than local contractors. They attempted to prove that their concrete would stay durable for a century and more. Samples of the fallen concrete were despatched back to Tokyo for analysis. Meanwhile, more concrete fell from the hotel's façade.

The hotel was closed for safety reasons. Langstreet continued to remain in his suite, even after the staff, all but a caretaker, had left.

Work on other constructions was halted.

The foundations of the Concord Hotel lay neglected, and filled with mud.

The bypass remained unfinished. Its attendant vehicles stood rusting, their gasoline siphoned off.

Kyriotisa lay open to the sun like a broken egg.

After many delays, the Japanese chemists reported that the blame for the deterioration of their concrete lay not with their formula but with the Greek workers on the building site. Although portable toilets – the ubiquitous Portaloos – had been provided, many workers had not bothered to use them, since the conveniences stood some distance away, on available ground. Instead, they had urinated into the cement mixers. Thus the concrete had been spoiled.

The local workers' union sued for malignant misrepresentation.

By June, the numbers of foreign visitors to the Kyriotisa shrine had fallen to just under two thousand. Many of those were journalists.

'WIND AND PISS: THE ANNA STORY!' was the headline in one German report.

One day before dawn, Archie Langstreet roused from sleep and smelt smoke. He padded to the apartment door and opened it. The upper hallway beyond was fuming. He heard a crackle of flame from below.

Calmly, he went to the phone and called the Hania fire brigade. Then he dipped a handkerchief under the bathroom tap, tied it round his face to cover nose and mouth, and retreated down the emergency stairs. The rear quarters of the hotel were alight. Langstreet stood helpless in his pyjamas in the cold dawn, looking on. The fire did not take, and was almost out when a fire engine arrived.

168

He insisted on entering the smouldering building with the fire chief. He found in the basement that the sprinkler system had never been connected to the water supply. Meanwhile, on the floor above, the fire chief was examining evidence for arson.

Langstreet went to the door in the back alley where Mr and Mrs Tsouderakis lived. Manolis let him in, invited him to sit on a kitchen chair, and gave him a Carter cigarette and a cup of coffee.

Mrs Tsouderakis came and smiled her bountiful smile at him, spreading wide her arms as if to express her dismay at the fire.

Langstreet did not complain. He sucked deeply on the cigarette and asked Tsouderakis if he would rent him a room for a few days.

'No, I am not able to do such a thing,' said the police chief.

'I do appreciate that there is a certain amount of hostility against me.'

Tsouderakis eyed him with an expression the other read as either irony or contempt.

'Hostility, you think? Mr Langstreet, you come to this quiet little town, you interfere in everything. You build things, you destroy things. You behave as your father has done. Now you have the place in a ruin and you think there is some hostility against you?!

'Let me tell you, Mr Langstreet, there is some hostility. There are many men in Kyriotisa who would like to kill you! No, you cannot stay with me. I will advise you get out of town, go. Stay away.'

Langstreet saw that his hand trembled as it rested on the table. He withdrew it to a place of concealment on his lap.

'I know our plans have gone wrong. My motives are unselfish, I can assure you. I hope to see Kyriotisa flourish. We'll soon get going again. I have the money – '

'Oh yes, you have the money. That gives you a right to mock our religion? To do what you will with our lives?'

He flinched as if from a blow. 'You misread the situation. I know – "You have the time, we have the money". But I am using my money to try to benefit you. You must believe that.'

'So why has it all gone wrong? You came in such a hurry. And, to explain, that expression is about watches, not time. It is a question of possessions. You thought you could buy up all Kyriotisa. It has angered people. So I advise you – get out of here!'

Langstreet drained his cup before standing up. 'Very well. Thank you for past support. I do understand you are disappointed. I will try to put things right.' He extended a hand.

Manolis Tsouderakis turned his back on it.

'History repeating itself,' said Langstreet. He nodded politely to the woman standing wiping her hands on her apron and left by the way he had come, into the alley.

At this stage, I had covered the north-east region of Crete, where most of the tourists stay. I had covered the Palace of Knossos. The Tourist Board of Iraklion had been helpful and provided me with photos for my book, as well as many brochures from which details went straight into my laptop. So I had moved westwards. I was staying in a pretty little hotel, The Lovos, in the Italian quarter of Hania.

Just for a day, I was taking it easy before doing the trip over the mountains southwards to Kyriotisa. It was not a visit to which I was looking forward.

Although self-pity has no part of my make-up, I wished life could be simple. In fact, I wished that a pleasant lady would enter my squalid room – naked except for maybe a bottle of vodka under her arm. I wished it so hard, I almost expected it to happen.

Nothing for it but to take a stroll. I had got talking to a nice French woman tourist. A certain mischievous expression about her lips and eyes had attracted me to sit at her table. We were seated at one of the pleasant restaurants which line the harbour front. Her name was Anne-Marie. She was on her own and staying in a hotel near me. A pretty and cultivated widow in her early fifties – my ideal. Sturdily built, with an immediately endearing swell of bosom under her blouse.

'You are a writer! Oh, that is so so romantic!'

'Not the way I do it.'

'Will you put me in your next book?'

'Mmm, depends how interesting you are…'

We were growing more intimate – she was admitting that her husband had run off with a young Netherlands boy, later committing suicide – and her pretty violet eyes with their false lashes were filling with tears – when I saw a familiar figure walking along the front. Was it? Yes, it was!

As I rose, making hasty excuses, Anne-Marie grasped my wrist. It was a firm, determined, clever grasp, so that for a moment I was back at university, playing cricket for my college, with a firm, determined, clever grasp of my bat, as I went in to score a century or a duck.

'Let's meet again. You interest me! My life is like a book!'

'Good – I long to hear everything. Hotel Lovos, Room 5.'

'D'accord!'

'Wiedersehen.'

Hurriedly, I went to catch up with Kathi Langstreet.

Although she gave me a smile, her face was lined and became grave and distant. I suggested that we sat at one of the café tables and talked.

She looked at her watch. She had managed to hire a car to take her to Kyriotisa. It would come for her in an hour. Nevertheless, she joined me at a gingham covered table, perching her behind on the edge of the chair. She sat looking out to sea, occasionally biting her lower lip as I talked.

After the waiter had served us two cappuccinos, she broke into what I was saying.

'I worry so about Archie.' She then told me a long story about the family finances. She had discovered that her husband had taken out a loan to pay for the expenses of Cliff and Vibe's wedding. This worried her greatly; they had never needed loans. She suspected that Archie had squandered a small fortune on the venture at Kyriotisa, rashly lending money here and there for which it was extremely unlikely he would ever receive any return. She protested that she was not a materialist; but to face old age in penury was a cause for anxiety. Finally, she looked me in the face and asked, 'Can't you do something?'

I shook my head. 'Archie has to act according to his character.'

Taking a packet of Carters from her handbag, Kathi inserted a cigarette between her red lips and lit it with a gold lighter.

'I didn't think you smoked, Kathi.'

She said, shortly, 'I'm acting out of character...' She exhaled and continued.

'He's such a good man. I admire Archie very much. He only wanted to leave his mark. He wanted to erase any bad local memories attached to his father's name. That's understandable, is it not? His character is extremely moral. Moral in a good sense.'

'Kathi, I'm no judge of these things, but Archie has turned the Anna cult – if you can call it that – into something spurious, something too big for its boots. He's built a theme park over a religious matter. Okay, he meant well. But he's, well, overambitious, wouldn't you say, to put it mildly?'

With a bitter look, she said, 'I know you don't like him. The promiscuous always dislike the principled.'

It would have been better to accept the snub in silence. There was truth in what she said. But I could not resist attempting a joke. 'You don't know the difficulties I have at my age. It's either chastity or adultery.' I added, 'Not too hard a choice, when you think about it.'

She took no notice. For a while she did not speak. With an expression of disgust, she stubbed out the remains of the cigarette in her saucer, as she launched into an attempt to explain how she had benefited from her husband's goodness in many ways. Archie, she repeated, had always been burdened by the past, and by his father's reputation. He really wished to make reparation. No, he was *driven* to make reparation. His demanding work for the legal side of the WHO had always been to that end. He had wanted to see peace and... Here she paused, before adding – peace and justice and decency in the world. He prayed for these things every night. He often made her pray with him.

'Once the burden of the lawsuit against Nentelstam was concluded – without success, unfortunately – and he retired, he was free to take on more altruistic...'

Her voice tailed away. She put an elbow on the table and rested her forehead in her hand. 'Oh, fuck!' she said to herself.

'It isn't that, is it?'

She looked angrily up at me. 'He's driven. He's all obsession. I can't get through to him any more. You understand? He always wished to make a name for himself – to be someone big, a benefactor – just to blot out the infamy of his father's name. It's tragic. Maybe his father was also a driven man...' She sighed. 'Archie's a man of principle, whatever you say.'

'Isn't it a sign of vanity to regard yourself as a man of principle?'

She ignored the remark.

'Of course, I can't help blaming myself. You know, I was weak. I think I told you that when I was young I was leading an immoral life – as Archie would see it – before I met him. By his example, I became a different person. He was abstemious, and strict with himself. I learnt that from him. I've tried to live by his rules.' She glanced at her watch without really looking at it. 'I suppressed all my wild side. I was faithful to him, always, always.'

'Does your Uncle Antal think that's a good idea?'

Again she ignored me.

Another little silence. Guessing at her mood, I said, 'Now you regret it? Now you see yourself growing old, with something in you left unexpressed which could have been expressed?'

173

'And if I had expressed it, then another aspect would have remained unexpressed instead. Isn't that so?' She glanced again at her watch. 'I must go. Why do I tell you these things? I know you are a – well, let's say, you are an amorous man. For some reason, to please your unprincipled mind, I don't know, for some reason you want me to say I am now amorous, that maybe I regret not living a more libidinous life. That's not quite the case. I'm soon going to be driven to Kyriotisa to find my idiotic husband, to live out my life as – oh, as he wishes. Because I respect him, because he needs me. Because he has principles.'

I said rather sadly – perhaps more sadly than I felt, 'But to deny one's passionate life, that's not easy, is it?'

With a smile, looking out to sea again, she replied that I was trying to read her mind. And getting it wrong.

As so often when confronted by something serious, I tried to turn it into a joke.

'You know the old chestnut about how to impress your lover? It turns on the relative simplicity of men, as compared with women.'

She sighed and glanced at her watch, but I persevered.

'To impress a woman, a man must do many things. Compliment her, kiss her, protect and care for her, listen to her – that's the hardest part – and adore her. Whereas, if a woman wants to impress a man, she just has to turn up naked with a bottle of vodka under her arm.'

Kathi gave a short laugh, a ha without the second ha, and said she must go. Her car would be arriving by the fort.

'Be warned, you may find Kyriotisa in rather a terrible mess,' I told her, adding hastily, 'So I saw on television.'

'No worse than our finances…'

I took her hand and kissed it in French fashion. Kathi smiled sadly at me. Then she went on her way.

I would not meet her again. Obviously. This painful reflection was brought about, at least in part, by the knowledge that I, as author, experienced what the reader of a novel experiences, but perhaps more vividly, the action, the sorrow and gladness, as I acted out in spirit every role of every character in the book.

It was not hard to imagine that Kathi would find little comfort in Kyriotisa, a place brought to disaster by 'principles'. What do you expect?

That evening, I remained in my room in the Lovos Hotel, sobered by the thought of my departure from the scene. I had been reading the final chapter of *The Victor Hugo Club*, and was packing up my few possessions in preparation for an early start in the morning.

There came a knock at my door.

When I called for them to enter, in came Anne-Marie.

She was naked, and had a bottle of vodka under one arm.

AUTHOR'S NOTE

I am the true author of this novel. My disreputable old nameless author who features in these pages is not I.

Yet I am no longer the author who wrote the novel. For reasons I cannot explain here, my typescript of *Cretan Teat* languished in a publisher's office for over a year before being accepted for publication by the House of Stratus. It is not necessary to convey to you how this protracted delay afflicted me. Professional writers rely on regular publication; it is the way in which their writerly life is nourished. I was deprived of that nourishment.

Nevertheless, I continued to write. I continued to live. While I was writing this novel you hold, my state of mind was uncertain. I had suffered a severe blow in the previous year. I believe the novel reflects something of the tumult into which I was thrown. I would go so far as to say that I believed, even hoped, my life was at an end; silence from the first publisher's office reinforced that notion.

In the time that has elapsed, I have become calmer and less tormented. Many instants do make an eternity. I do not now recall clearly my desperation at that time. Of course, I am older. And I have become content again with life.

This is no apology for the wilder moments in *Cretan Teat*, which in some cases are echoes from my existence at that period. A writer with a continuing career is apt to regard all his books – however diverse they may appear to an outsider – as a continuous whole, a record of a mysterious inner life of which he is only in part aware. It is this continuity-within-change that is so valuable.

However, *Cretan Teat* was designed not merely for its reflections on an aspect of modern life, caught by its big toe in the past, but for – I would admittedly be bound to say this – amusement.

Brian Aldiss